FANFICTION

FAN FICTION

A Mem-Noir
Inspired by True Events

BRENT SPINER

WITH
JEANNE DARST

ST. MARTIN'S PRESS
NEW YORK

First published in the United States by St. Martin's Press, an imprint of St. Martin's Publishing Group

FAN FICTION. Copyright © 2021 by Brent Spiner. All rights reserved. Printed in the United States of America. For information, address St. Martin's Publishing Group, 120 Broadway, New York, NY 10271.

www.stmartins.com

Endpapers designed by Rob Grom; patterns © local_doctor/Shutterstock.com; lips © Svetalik/Shutterstock.com

Library of Congress Cataloging-in-Publication Data
Names: Spiner, Brent, author.
Title: Fan fiction : a mem-noir inspired by true events / Brent Spiner.
Description: First edition. | New York : St. Martin's Press, 2021.
Identifiers: LCCN 2021026587 | ISBN 9781250274366 (hardcover) |
    ISBN 9781250280640 (signed) | ISBN 9781250274373 (ebook)
Subjects: LCSH: Spiner, Brent—Fiction. | Motion picture industry—
    Fiction. | Fame—Fiction. | Fans (Persons)—Fiction. | Star Trek
    fiction. | LCGFT: Autobiographical fiction.
Classification: LCC PS3619.P5639 F36 2021 | DDC 813/.6—dc23
LC record available at https://lccn.loc.gov/2021026587

Our books may be purchased in bulk for promotional, educational, or business use. Please contact your local bookseller or the Macmillan Corporate and Premium Sales Department at 1-800-221-7945, extension 5442, or by email at MacmillanSpecialMarkets@macmillan.com.

First Edition: 2021

10 9 8 7 6 5 4 3 2 1

To my mother—for a lifetime of love and support
and for always being my biggest fan

CONTENTS

fan fiction *n.* fiction, usually fantasy or science fiction, written by a fan rather than a professional author, *esp.* that based on already-existing characters from a television series, book, film, etc.; (also) a piece of such writing.

—OXFORD DICTIONARY

FANFICTION

PROLOGUE

WHEN I WAS twenty-two years old, I left home for the first time and departed for New York City along with a meager cache of savings and the dream of being an actor. Traveling by train from Houston to Chicago to Buffalo and then down into Manhattan, I arrived on New Year's Eve 1972 and took a room for the night at the New York Hilton on Sixth Avenue. At around eleven, I walked to Times Square, where there seemed to be at least a million people huddled together on Broadway and Seventh Avenue. It was freezing that night, about 1 degree Fahrenheit, but I didn't even feel it. I had arrived! I was going to take the New York theater world by storm! When the legendary New Year's Ball dropped at the stroke of midnight, I hugged and kissed absolute strangers. It was a very heady experience. I went back to the hotel, went to sleep, and woke up in the morning with a 102-degree fever, compliments of a catastrophic case of the flu. I was sick for a solid month. A friend of my brother's, Dennis Hanovich, a saint, allowed me to stay in his guest room while I recovered.

After a few weeks, I couldn't take it anymore. I'd been in the Big Apple for almost a month and had seen nothing of it other than the inside of Dennis's guest room. "What are you doing?" I said to myself. "Get up! Go out! Take a look at New York City!" I dragged myself out of bed, pulled on my clothes, took the elevator to the ground floor, and walked out onto West End Avenue. I gasped. It was like a fairy tale, a WINTER WONDERLAND! The snow had been falling all day, and the city was wrapped in a blanket of white. Exhilarated, I decided to stroll a few blocks and enjoy this new adventure. But soon I thought better of it. "You're still sick. Be smart. Go back to bed."

As I turned to go back to the apartment, every light on West End Avenue went out. There was a complete blackout. It was so cold that at almost the same instant, one of my lenses popped out of my glasses. I looked for it, but with only one good eye, I couldn't spot it in the snow and the total darkness. Removing one of my gloves, I began feeling for it, but I still couldn't find it. So I took off the other glove and swept the snow with both hands, hoping one of my fingers would make contact with it. Nothing! Then I got down on my knees in the damp powder and frantically made angel wings in the snow with my hands. Nothing. At that very moment, a taxicab swept by, its tires sending a tidal wave of wet slush over my entire body. Now I was wet and sick and I wanted to go home. Feeling completely defeated, I thought, *What am I doing here?*

I can't make it in New York. I can't even stay alive here! I looked up to the heavens, snowflakes dotting my face, and cried out, "God! Should I go back to Houston? Give me a sign!" And then my other lens popped out. "Thanks, God. Thanks a lot," I said. But then a strange thing happened. A warm and wonderful feeling passed through me, and I knew what it was. Hypothermia! I was freezing to death. No! No, that wasn't it at all. It was defiance! I whipped off my empty frames, threw them in the snow, and shouted to the indifferent world around me, "You can't beat me, New York! I'll conquer you yet!" I was certain of my path, and I would never give up.

My first apartment, a one-room studio on the ground floor, was on West 80th Street between Amsterdam and Broadway. It was right around the corner from Zabar's, which was the only good thing about it. The bathroom was so small that the door, when open, hit the toilet, making it only possible to enter like a crab, sliding in sideways. I was able, with my savings, to equip my new digs with a secondhand bed, a tiny couch, and most important, a portable TV. The night after I bought it, I came home from a walk, opened the apartment door, and found the place completely bare. No bed, no couch, and most distressingly, no TV. Fortunately, the thieves found my clothes unacceptable. Those were the days of New York's "mean streets," and they were decidedly unfriendly to me. I was mugged a couple of times and I couldn't get arrested in the theater.

The only acting job I had in that first year was as an impostor on the game show *To Tell the Truth*. I pretended to be a cabdriver from Denver who played trumpet requests for his customers. No one on the panel of celebrities voted for me; hence I made no money. But I did meet Nipsey Russell, so it wasn't a total loss. And inspired by my cabdriving charade, I got my hack license. The requirements to drive a cab in New York in those days were pretty simple. There was a quiz in which you had to know eight very common locations such as Radio City Music Hall, Times Square, etc. Any tourist could ace this test. Before being rewarded with your license, however, one had to be checked out by a "doctor" in Queens. I was instructed to drop my trousers and underwear, turn my head, and cough while he cradled my cojones for what seemed like an inordinate amount of time. That was the extent of the examination.

Eventually, my luck began to turn. I landed a few small roles in off-Broadway productions. In time, the parts got bigger and better and I graduated to the occasional Broadway show. Most impressively, I played Aramis in the 1984 revival of Rudolf Friml's operetta *The Three Musketeers*, which lasted a week and lost twelve million dollars. Though financially I was barely getting by, I didn't care. I was a paid actor. Then the IRS summoned me to their offices. I hadn't paid my taxes ("what are taxes?") and I owed the government $4,000. Since I had nothing more than my last paycheck in the bank, about $700, I was certain a jail cell was in my future. And then providence raised its beautiful head. A relative of mine had died—not so fortunate for him, I guess—and had made me the beneficiary of an insurance policy that paid out exactly $4,000. Crazy how things sometimes work out. But I was still broke.

About this time, I got my first role in a film. I think it's fair to call it a film. A cut-rate Italian company came to New York to make an "American comedy" titled *Rent Control*. The director had seen me in a play and was certain I was perfect for the lead role, a schnook who scoured the obituaries hoping to find a rent-controlled apartment previously occupied by someone who was recently deceased. Little by little I put together that this was a mob-financed venture. My salary checks were signed by an obstetrician in New Jersey. When the movie was completed, it played for a couple of days at the Waverly Theater in the Village to a combined audience of about six and a half people. The entire budget of the film was $100,000, but to the director's credit, it looked like $200,000. Though it did nothing for my career, it did allow me to put some money in the bank. I was thirty-four and growing very weary of living like a teenager, so I decided, with this one questionable film credit, to give Hollywood a try. I scored a job as a replacement, playing Seymour Krelborn in the original West Coast production of *Little Shop of Horrors*, and said goodbye to New York. The show lasted only another three weeks, but it allowed me to secure an agent and, with luck and perseverance, find my way into guest-starring roles and TV movies.

And then *Star Trek: The Next Generation* happened. I auditioned for the role of the android Data six times. Apparently they weren't sure I was the guy for the part, and frankly, I wasn't sure I wanted to be tied down to a series. I was doing pretty well at this point and enjoying playing a variety of characters. But finally they offered me the role, and I figured what the hell, it couldn't last more than a season and I could make some decent money. And the rest is history. My history, anyway. Immediately after I was hired, Gene Roddenberry, the creator of the show, said something to me I'll never forget. "Your life will never be the same." I had no idea what he meant at the time, but he couldn't have been more correct. So many wonderful experiences began to unfold for me. I had a challenging role to grapple with, I was making a decent income, and I was working with some talented and wonderful people.

And then something truly unbelievable happened. Something I can describe only as a slapstick nightmare occurred in the fourth season of the show and gave Gene's words a completely different context.

Everything I have written thus far is absolutely true. But the story I'm about to tell is not. In fact, having written the book and read it a few times, I'm not sure if any of it really happened. Maybe in a parallel universe?

ONE

PANDORA'S BOX

THE SECOND WORST part of my job is wearing makeup. The worst is taking it off. The only thing that will cut through my thick mask at the end of a sixteen-hour day is a kerosene-based product called Eliminate. In case you missed it, I said *kerosene*. I've doubtless swallowed at least a gallon of the stuff in an attempt to rid myself of every fleck of gold powder that has worked its way into the pores and orifices of my head. If anything is being "eliminated," it's several layers of skin and the well-being of a couple of internal organs, brain cells, and potentially essential fifteen-years-down-the-road sperm. But hey, the show must go on.

While I am going through my end-of-the-day ritual in the two-by-two bathroom of my trailer, which is the exact size of an airplane bathroom and just as comfortable, a knock comes at the open door, followed by the familiar voice of Mickey, the mailroom boy. "Package for you, Mr. S."

Wiping the excess lighter fluid from my face with a never-again-to-be-used towel, my eyes burning thanks to the flesh-melting Eliminate, I stumble to the door. My trailer is one of a breed of what are called honeywagons, and a second-rate version at that, especially reserved for syndicated series. Originally designed in the early twentieth century for animal stars, they're strictly utilitarian structures to say the least, though admittedly, they're considerably nicer than my old apartment in New York. Mickey loiters outside the door holding a large cardboard box and wearing a ridiculous expression on his face. He stands just under five feet and has almost white-blond hair and skin the same color. If they ever start making vampire movies in this town again, this kid could be a star. Though he delivers the mail to nicer trailers than mine, he's still a bit of a fan and usually genuflects when not carrying such a large package. I'm thankful that on this occasion the size of the carton prevents any such embarrassing display.

"Gotta love those fans, Mr. S. This feels like something important . . . though I gotta say, it don't smell very good," he says, taking a huge whiff.

I don't care for the sound of that.

"In the future, Mickey," I admonish him, "if a package comes for me, and it doesn't smell very good . . ."

"I know," he butts in, "spray it with Right Guard before I bring it to you. That shit'll take the stink outta anything. I ought to know."

Not wishing to pursue the matter, I swallow the rest of my sentence. Mickey takes the two steps up into my trailer, and as he crosses the threshold, the aroma hits me. It is so heinous, so revolting, it can be described only as a solid. It's like getting a left hook to the olfactory nerve. There is something unmistakable about it. It is the smell of . . . evil. He plunks it down on the foldout table that doubles as office and dining room in my home away from home. I can't actually get close enough to open it. The smell is like an invisible shield between me and the box.

"Yeah, it's kind of stinky," says Mickey.

I'm not sure what disturbs me more, the smell or the fact that he finds it "kind of stinky." Getting woozy, I stagger outside, followed by Mickey.

"Well, if you need anything I'll be here till midnight," he says, reaching out to shake my hand.

"Uh . . . Thanks, Mick," I say, and slip him a ten-dollar bill very carefully, so as not to touch the hand that held that vile box. "Enjoy your evening. Full moon, you know."

It's one of those Los Angeles nights when a marine layer covers the moon like Vaseline over a camera lens.

"Oooh, yeah," he says, flashing a couple of pearly whites that could cut through an oil drum, "my kinda night!"

And he wolf-howls like Lon Chaney Jr.—I swear he does—before disappearing into the mist. Paramount Pictures in 1991 is lousy with nutty characters.

Deciding to take another shot at opening the box, I inhale a few deep breaths and start in. But my good sense coupled with the atrocious odor stops me cold.

"What if there's something alive in there?" I say to myself.

I chew on that thought for a couple of seconds and then sprint next door to see if LeVar Burton is still in his trailer.

All of the cast on *The Next Generation* have become good friends in a very short time. Series work will do that. Or it will do the opposite. The long hours and repetitive work either forge lifelong mates or create bitter enemies. My relationship with LeVar was cemented by the birth of his daughter, Michaela. He showed up at my door not long after the blessed event with a jar containing the placenta, asking me to keep it in my freezer until he and his wife, Stephanie, moved into their new home. Apparently their own freezer was spiritually contaminated, as it was housing a few pounds of beef in various states of dissection. Their intention was to eventually bury the placenta in a hole along with a newly planted apple tree. And that's exactly what they did. The last time I visited their house, I was delighted to see the tree had grown tall and strong, with apples that all looked curiously like Michaela's head.

LeVar's trailer is the antithesis of mine. It is filled with dozens of crystals and the intoxicating, unmistakable perfume of patchouli and lavender, mixed with the residue of Export 'A' cigarettes. I call it LeVaroma. The lavender, by the way, is reputed to keep evil spirits away, so I'm definitely in the right place. LeVar sits on his sofa with his legs tucked under him in a pretzel-like configuration. His eyes are closed and his breathing suggests some secret mantra running over and over through his mind. As much as I hate to disturb him, I figure that if he is in a transcendental state, he will surely forgive me.

"Burt . . ."

He told me once that Steve McQueen called him Burt when they made the movie *The Hunter*. He said I was like McQueen in that way. In every other way—well, not so much.

"Burt . . . I know you're in there somewhere. If you can hear me, I need your help."

He peels one eye open, then the other. He looks like a giant bird slowly coming to life. Very, very slowly, or so it feels to me. At last, after a long series of deep inhalations through his nose, he speaks.

"Do you know where I keep my pistol?" he says like a character in some other movie.

"No. You have a pistol?"

"No," he whispers as an enigmatic smile crosses his face. The Mona Lisa has nothing on LeVar. "What's the problem?"

"This is going to sound ridiculous, but there's a box . . . do you really have a pistol?"

"No." Again the enigmatic smile.

"Anyway, Mickey just delivered a box to me that smells like . . . like . . ." My hands and face contort to express just how awful it is.

"Like evil?"

"Something in the evil family, yes," I say, not at all surprised at LeVar's intuition.

He untwists his limbs and sweeps a black saddlebag up from the floor. He reaches into one of the pockets and withdraws a long stalk of some kind of dried plant.

"This is sage," he says. "It's used to eliminate negative energy. Evil spirits. Let's go smudge that motherfucker."

Before we brave my unholy lair, LeVar strikes a match and sets the sage on fire. He lets it burn a few seconds and then blows it out. And as pungent smoke continues to billow from its tip, he passes it over the length of my trailer.

"Will that do it?" I whimper, buying into hocus-pocus for the first time in my life.

"That just lets them know we're here."

We open the door and peek our heads in, as if we're doing a remake of *Abbott and Costello Meet Frankenstein*. LeVar is one step into the trailer when the smell hits him. It literally knocks him to the ground.

"I'm not going in there," he says as he picks himself up off the ground. "You need more than sage for that evil stink."

He makes a fast U-turn for the safety of his crystal palace, with this born-again believer on his heels.

"You got something stronger, Burt?" I ask, now certain he has a voodoo spell that will do the trick.

"Yeah. I'm calling Paramount security."

As is typical in an emergency, help arrives half an hour later, in the person of Ted Spiegel, studio security chief, the Lone Ranger in a white golf cart with the *William Tell* Overture playing in a continual loop in his brain. If he could wear a mask, he would. He dismounts—if it's actually possible to dismount from a golf cart—and marches fearlessly to the door of my trailer.

"Stand back, boys," he commands as he charges in.

We do. Several feet. Even at that distance, the putrid aroma makes its way to our nostrils. Ted seems oblivious.

"How can you stand it, Ted?" I call to him as I back another few feet away.

"I got hit by a car when I was seventeen," he says, pulling a Rambo-like knife from a scabbard attached to his belt. "Lost my sense of smell. Best thing that ever happened to me."

He slices open the top of the box like he's performing surgery and carefully looks inside. He lets out one of those "holy shit" kind of whistles. Then he picks up the box and tilts it toward us so we can appreciate what he has just seen. The sides of the box are lined with heavy plastic, which is a good thing, because inside is some horrible fleshy object, floating in blood.

"What the hell is that?" I manage to croak.

"That, gentlemen, is a pig's penis," says Ted.

"Au jus," adds LeVar, ever the wit.

I would laugh if what I was looking at wasn't so horribly, bloodily, grotesquely real.

"I'm not sure I want the answer to this, Ted, but how do you know?"

A strange, dark memory passes over Ted's face for what seemed like a long holiday weekend.

"I once saw a man lying facedown with his arms and legs tied behind him. One of these babies was stuck down his throat."

They say acting isn't acting, it's reacting. LeVar and I are paralyzed. Neither of us know exactly what in God's name to say, but I take a leap. "Was he dead?"

The way Ted looks at me makes it clear I am not the straight man of this comedy team. "That man was my uncle Sam," he confides, as if we want to know.

"Jesus" is all LeVar can get out.

"Yeah, Jesus," says Ted with a disgust that tells us his churchgoing days are far behind him.

He tilts the box so that LeVar and I can see the underside of the lid where the word DEAD is written in black marker. Dead. LeVar looks at me as if to say, "I can't sage this but it's going to be okay." Nice try, but I don't feel like it's going to be okay.

Still lost in his own nightmare, Ted shuts the box and lifts it into his arms, leaves my honeywagon, slides back into his saddle, and drives away. I wish that I could drive away on some company-owned white golf cart, home to Ted's word-jumble-doing wife and his over-air-conditioned ranch house in Toluca Lake. I wish I could sleep the sleep of Ted, an older man with nothing to wrestle with, nothing to hide from or cover up, no makeup or lines to learn. No one is out there following his golf cart; no one is concealed behind a window watching him or waiting at his house for him to come home alone. Or sending him blood-soaked genitalia. No one wants him dead.

TWO

DEAR DADDY

AFTER A SLEEPLESS night, I arrive the next morning at the studio and make my way as slowly as possible to my trailer. This walk has filled me with joy since my first day on the show. Passing the dressing room buildings of Bob Hope and Bing Crosby and countless other Paramount stars always makes me feel that I have arrived, literally and figuratively. But on this morning, a sense of dread fills my soul. Arriving at my honeywagon, I hesitate before daring to open the door. Has the evil smell gone away with the package? Finally, with enormous trepidation, I crack the door and take a sniff. No, dammit, it still smells rancid. Holding my breath, I flap the door open and shut like the wing of a giant seagull, then dash inside, open the windows, and turn on a fan. Something on the floor catches my eye—a white envelope. It wasn't here before, was it? Did it come with the package?

Reluctantly I pick the envelope up off the floor. On it is written BRENT SPINER in careful, neat handwriting, with the

Paramount address underneath my name. No return address. A strange sensation sprouts in my stomach, similar to being strapped into a roller coaster, slowly climbing upward, looking forward but not being able to see over the edge. Tearing open the envelope, I withdraw the letter inside. More meticulous handwriting:

> *Dear Daddy,*
>
> *Why have you forsaken me? I thought you loved me. I am so alone here. Is this heaven? Or is it hell?*
> *Won't you join me? I think I can make that happen.*
> *I'm so tired of waiting for you.*
> *Soon, Daddy, very soon.*
>
> *Your loving daughter,*
> *Lal*

As I read the name *Lal,* I'm seeing over the edge of that roller coaster, this time on its way down, a long way down. This dizzying disturbance is accompanied by that terrifying feeling in the pit of your stomach when you have a betrayal of the bowels and you might not make it in time. It's like a scene in a film when the camera zooms in and dollies out at the same time, a radical, surreal change of perception indicating extreme confusion and fear, as if a sneak attack by this individual could happen at any moment. A cold sweat breaks out on my forehead. What is the significance of the name Lal, you might ask. You wouldn't know unless you are familiar with the episode of *Star Trek: The Next Generation* titled "The Off-spring." More on that later. But first, the PS:

I hope you liked my little gift. Be sure to show it to Riker at Nickodell on Friday? Anyway, it reminded me of you.

Nickodell is a restaurant, built in 1936, that operates right outside the Paramount gates. Many of the cast and crew end up at its winding, polished mahogany bar on Friday nights after work for a martini or two before heading home for the weekend. It's one of those classic Hollywood joints, dimly lit, with seascapes and velvet nude paintings adorning the walls. We love it. But apparently last Friday night someone else was there. Someone watching me, stalking me. Someone plotting to horrify me with a sick surprise. And possibly worse.

THREE   *NIGHTHAWKS*

MIDNIGHT. LYING IN my bed, awake in the dark and for some unknown reason, thinking about my stepfather, Sol, who married my mother when I was seven. Sol was a stylish clotheshorse and an enthusiastic dancer who was handsome in an Alec Baldwin-y sort of way. He and my mother spent many an evening cha-chaing on the waxed floor of the Club Crescendo. My biological father, Jack, who tragically passed away when I was ten months old, was more of a cigar and poker sort of guy. He was also very handsome. My mother says he looked kind of like Elvis and that everyone loved him.

Mom believed that every boy needed a father, so her decision to marry Sol a few years after my father's death was motivated by what she felt was best for my brother, Ronnie, and me. Also, it didn't hurt that he was good-looking.

The only problem was that Sol was a sociopath. He demanded order in the house at all times, and nothing was ever neat enough to please him. I'm talking about military neat. Flip a coin on the bed neat. Because of minor infractions involving anything from food in the sink to leaving our shoes under the bed, Ronnie and I were grounded for four out of the six years Sol lived with us. We were prisoners in our own house, trapped with a sadistic maniac who got some bizarre, twisted kind of pleasure from controlling every aspect of our lives. We rarely if ever felt safe. Whenever Sol was in the house, danger was lurking around each corner, always ready to pounce. I was terrified of him. And since then, I've been afraid of almost everything. Maybe that's why I became an actor. I didn't want to feel afraid anymore. I wanted to feel loved . . . by the world. I thought being loved meant being safe. Looks like the joke's on me.

Drifting off to sleep, I dissolve into an involuntary world . . .

A rainy night in an unnamed city. A diner, Edward Hopper's Nighthawks. *Inside, the counter is empty but for one lone figure, my stepfather, Sol. He turns his back to me and I can see over his shoulder that he's looking at a photo, an actor's headshot. My headshot. In the photo, I'm about twenty-five and smiling that goofy "I need a job" sort of smile. A server arrives in the form of a pinkish-gold, featureless, genderless android with a Louise Brooks black bob, pen and notepad in hand, ready to take Sol's order. He shows the pink android the photo of me and whispers something to her that I can't hear. The android sees me through the window and points straight toward me. Sol turns around and looks at me. He is not smiling. In fact, he's furious.*

I bolt awake in a cold sweat. No doubt, cold sweat is going to become a constant theme in my life. I look at the clock: one A.M. The rest of the night I stare at the ceiling and wonder what Sol said to the alien.

FOUR THE HEAD OF OBSESSIVES

THE FOLLOWING DAY, I meet with Ted, the Paramount head of security, whose office is cluttered with unfinished business and dozens of empty wrappers of Peanut Butter Kandy Kakes. I show him the letter I found in my trailer, and for a few seconds he doesn't speak. Then he snaps his fingers and smiles that "I've seen things you don't want to know about" smile. He scribbles something on a piece of paper and hands it to me: a police department address with the title *Head of Obsessives*.

"His name is Ortiz. I've known him a long while. He owes me one. When I was a cop, he was my masseur. Magic hands. I swear—no one could get a knot out of my buttocks better than him!"

He pauses and gets that faraway look in his eyes again. I assume he's remembering a particularly good rubdown. Or something.

"Wasn't really making ends meet, so to speak, so I got him into the academy. Smart guy, great detective. He moved up quick!"

Happily leaving his office, I hop into my trusty Toyota Corolla and drive to the police station downtown, the vibe there reminding me of the TV show *Hill Street Blues*. I did an episode of that series when I first got to Hollywood, and only now do I appreciate how good their sets were.

I approach a desk sergeant. "Excuse me, I'm looking for . . ."

I peruse the writing on the piece of paper given to me by Ted. I feel kind of silly saying this out loud, but I forge ahead. "I'm looking for . . . the head of obsessives."

"Yeah, Ortiz, he's in Behavioral Sciences, Threat Management. Eighth floor. Elevator's over there."

Minutes later I'm shaking hands with a fiftyish bearish, boisterous detective with huge hands and an unkempt handlebar moustache that clearly has no sense of direction. Edward James Olmos gets the part in the movie. Behind him are framed citations and diplomas, most related to police and detective work except for a masseur's license and a signed photo of Truman Capote with the inscription *To Ortiz! You had me at "turn over"!*

"Mr. Spiner, my goodness, please sit down. Why don't you start at the beginning?"

"I received this letter," I say as I pull the envelope out of my backpack and offer it to him. "It arrived with a rotting pig penis floating in a container of blood."

"Yes . . . Paramount security filled me in on the pig penis." His face contorts slightly with a look that combines both disgust and curiosity. "That's disgusting . . . and curious. Put the letter on the desk, please."

As with all authority figures, I obey. The head of obsessives opens a drawer and retrieves a pair of disposable latex gloves. "In case there are any fingerprints."

Hadn't thought of that. Careless of me. He delicately peels open the envelope, removes the letter, and begins to read out loud with surprising feeling. "'Dear Daddy . . . Why have you forsaken me . . . I thought you loved me . . . I am so alone here . . . Is this heaven . . . Or is it hell . . . Won't you join me . . . I think I can make that happen . . . I'm so tired of waiting for you . . . Soon, Daddy, very soon . . . Your loving daughter . . . Lal.'"

The head of obsessives puts the letter down, nods his brilliantined head, and observes: "Fascinating. Well, one thing we know, whoever it is, they're a copycat."

"Copycat?"

"That's right. A Lal copycat."

"You know who Lal is?" I ask.

"Sure I do. She was your daughter on *Star Trek*. Until she tragically suffered a complete mental breakdown and died."

I wasn't expecting him to know about any of this. Kind of cool. The head of obsessives watches the show.

"I'm actually a big fan . . . I guess I'm more a fan of Data than of you, 'cause I don't really know your other stuff. I just know the character you play on the show."

"You ever watch *Hill Street Blues*? I played a porno director . . ."

He ignores me and charges ahead. "That was one of my favorite episodes, 'The Offspring.' And, may I say, very sensitively directed by Mr. Frakes. Your character, the android Data, desires to have a child. So he creates one in a cybernetics laboratory, another humanoid android he names Lal, the Hindi word for beloved. At first Lal looks very strange— pinkish gold, genderless, mostly featureless. But soon Data chooses her humanoid form, that of a young woman. Amusingly, he tries to teach his daughter how to assimilate into the society and culture of the *Enterprise*. Captain Picard is concerned about this new life-form, and in the B story, Starfleet Admiral Haftel arrives and declares that he is taking Lal away for further study. Data refuses to cooperate with this request. This debate is quickly put aside because of a massive malfunction in Lal's brain, a cascade failure that threatens to end her new life. Data tries to save his daughter but fails, and she dies. Tragic. In the end, Data downloads Lal's memories into his own mind, keeping his memories of her forever close. Cried like a baby the first time I watched it."

Okay, I decide, maybe Ortiz is even more than a fan. He continues:

"It's apparent this individual is playing the role of Lal after she died on the show. In this scenario, she's trapped in your mind, which has become a kind of limbo or purgatory for her. And she wants you to join her there, whatever that really means. In death, maybe. I don't get the significance of the pig penis, though. Perhaps she wants to castrate you as a form of patricide?"

"Castrate me? Patricide?"

"Cutting off the penis of the father. To kill him. Very common."

"Oh God." I'm getting the roller-coaster and gurgling

stomach sensation combined with cold sweat again. A very real stalker believes she's my "forsaken" android daughter, trapped as memories in my own brain? It's all too much to take in. I just want to work. Ply my trade. Get a little worldwide adulation. Nothing like this! A dark tunnel emerges around the head of obsessives.

"Mr. Spiner, are you okay? You don't look well."

"I don't feel well."

"It's gonna be fine. Lemme give you an analogy. Let's say you're Data on the *Enterprise,* after Lal has died. One day a pig penis is delivered through the transporter, with a letter for Data that says, 'Dear Daddy, why have you forsaken me, I thought you loved me, I am so alone here . . .'"

"All right, all right, I get it. Please stop saying those words."

"So what does Data do? He wants to find out who this person is and why this person is doing what they're doing. All he's gotta do is put his mind into Lal's mind, think just like her—or him—to figure out who she or he is and stop her or him. It's a puzzle, just like the ones Data solves all time on *The Next Generation.* Too bad you're not actually Data! Ha!"

It's impossible to share his laugh. But he's right. Too bad, indeed. He goes on.

"We just have to be careful not to do anything that sets off this Lal. That could make things worse. Also, the PS section of the letter, 'I hope you liked my little gift. Be sure to show it to Riker at Nickodell on Friday,' indicates that she—or he—knows where you hang out, and is spying on you, either in person or with the use of a proxy. Which means there's a chance that you already know this person. You just don't know if she—or he—is also this person. And she or he could even have an accomplice, which you also may or may not know. So, to put it succinctly, we don't know shit."

I bury my face in my hands and groan. *Mmmmgggmmm.* In my mind, I see the ghostly figure from Edvard Munch's *The Scream.* Except he looks like me.

"You seem tense, Mr. Spiner. May I call you Brent?"

"Whatever," I mumble. But I can't see the head of obsessives. Just the darkness inside my own hands, as if I'm trapped in a dark, fleshy cage.

I hear Ortiz stand and walk behind me. His two strong paws grasp my trapezius muscles. The head of obsessives is massaging my shoulders. It's making me feel more than a little creeped out, but oddly, slightly more relaxed at the same time. He whispers from behind my head.

"By the way, I've written a great spec script for a *Star Trek* episode with Data. He goes back in time to the twentieth century and teams up with a brilliant Hispanic detective to track down a serial killer. I'll give you a copy. Maybe you can . . ."—his fingers burrow hard into a tender knot at the back of my neck—"interest someone at Paramount in it."

Emitting another pained groan, I think about how yesterday a stalker sent me a pig penis, and today I'm getting a massage from the detective who's supposed to save me from that stalker. Still, I have to agree with Ted: this cat has magic hands.

FIVE

MY TRANSFORMATION INTO Data begins first thing in the morning as I struggle to insert yellow contacts into my eyes. It usually takes twenty or thirty attempts, but the joy of eventual success is inestimable. Except for the pain, of course. Kind of feels like I've got fingernail clippings attached to my pupils. And although these lenses were made specifically for me, in my own prescription, I can barely see through them. They turn me into a sort of intergalactic Mr. Magoo. I stumble to the makeup trailer and into the chair of the great artist Michael Westmore, who proceeds to pack a pound of phosphorescent powder onto my punim. Michael is currently the reigning monarch of the legendary family, the Westmores of Hollywood, who basically invented the makeup business for movies. There was a time when the head of the makeup department at every studio in town was a Westmore. I doubt it's much of a thrill for him to turn a Texas Jew into an android from Omicron Theta, but I get goose bumps every day just being part of his history. Two chairs down, Michael Dorn, my friend and castmate, pores over the morning's crossword puzzle, having just been remade by Westmore's magic into his renowned Klingon persona, Worf.

"Mike, aside from Dorny, who's the most difficult actor you ever made up?"

Without hesitation he offered: "Easy. Bette Davis. She used to grab the pencil out of my hand while I was doing her brows. She'd say, 'No, like this!' And she'd pull the pencil across her forehead like she was striking a match. 'That's how you do eyebrows!' she'd shriek. They looked ridiculous. Bitch."

"How about that, Dorny?" I say, throwing him a sideways glance. "You and Bette Davis. Pretty cool."

Without looking up from his paper, he slowly growls: "What's an eight-letter word for *garrote*?"

"Well, let me see, uh, *strangle*?"

There is a long pause while I absorb his intent. I'm relieved to note a slight upward curl at the corners of his mouth. These days, I tend to take things a lot more seriously. Turning back to the mirror, I watch the face of Brent disappear and the golden visage of Data gradually emerge. With each blink, the powder dislodges, floats into my eyes, and smears across my lenses, leaving me just this side of legally blind. That's when my anxiety escalates a notch. Although the porcine prick and the threatening letter have motivated Paramount security to step up the high measures already in place around the set, making the *Enterprise* the safest place in the galaxy, I'm not completely reassured. What if Lal somehow gets past security and onto the set? I won't even be able to see her—or him—coming.

All day long I work in a nervous daze, but the hyperrational Data keeps pulling me through. The calm that envelops me when I assume his persona is like a balm to my tortured soul. I ask myself, "How would he react to this situation?" and I answer in his voice: "Analyze the problem. Search for abnormal patterns. Use the information to make an assessment and respond accordingly. Do not let fear lead you to irrational decisions." Data will be my guide.

I have so much on my mind that the cycle of performing, waiting around, and then performing again is particularly grueling. After a typical sixteen hours, we finally wrap up the workday. I'm eager to remove these contacts so at least I'll be able to see if Lal is coming toward me.

As I walk outside between the trailers, an unfamiliar voice calls out from a distance: "Hey, Data!"

Did he say Data? Or was it Daddy? I pretend not to hear and walk faster. Could it be Lal?

"Wait up!"

I start to jog. Suddenly I feel the presence of a man at my side, moving even faster than I am. He steps in front of me and blocks my forward motion. Lifting my hands into a defensive posture, I squint through blurred vision at the looming shadow before me.

"What the hell do you want?" I squeak timidly.

"Brent, I just want to say how honored I am to be working with you on the show. Really."

An embarrassed breath escapes from my solar plexus as I recognize the voice of an actor appearing in a small role in the episode we're currently shooting. "Well, hey, uh, great!" I say, foolishly grabbing his hand and pumping it like a maniac. "Excellent work today," I lie.

I didn't even have a scene with him, for God's sake!

"This is my first job in six months," he confesses, "and to end that dry spell by working on this show, it's just really . . ."

I sense him laying a hand on the center of his chest.

". . . heartening. It's so inspiring to be working with an actor of your caliber."

Like I said, I didn't have any scenes with him.

"Well, thanks . . . uh . . ."

"Todd."

"Todd, sure, right . . . Todd! Well, Todd, I hope this leads to lots of good things for you," I bullshit. At last I take pity on both of us and release his hand from my sweaty grip.

His ebullient voice turns quieter and a hint of melancholy creeps into it. "Six months ago my wife left me. Money's been really tight. So it's just amazing to be welcomed on board the *Enterprise*. It's like being lifted from a bottomless pit and deposited onto a beautiful spaceship. And you know what's really weird? I auditioned for your role back in '86. If I'd gotten it instead of you, my life would've been completely different."

There it is. The motive. A frightening thought rekindles in my mind. Am I, destitute of vision, gazing at my own stalker? I remember the advice from the head of obsessives: Don't do anything to set Lal off. Just be cool and give him a smile. Cool is not really in my repertoire, though smiling insincerely is right up my alley. I don't say anything but just keep grinning at him, trying to remember what his face looks like. I may have to identify him in a police lineup one day.

"Well, I guess you're eager to get out of that makeup," he says. "I'm working again on Friday. See you then."

He claps my shoulder and disappears toward the Melrose Gate. I'm relieved he's not going to make his move tonight, but my mind is racing. Is he just an underemployed actor kissing my ass? Or is he actually my daughter, Lal? I mean . . . you know what I mean. I gotta get these contacts out. Maybe I'll see things more clearly when I can . . . see things more clearly.

✳

Arriving safely back at my trailer, I immediately notice the door is ajar. Strange? I'm certain I closed it tightly when I left. My heart is beating in my throat as I crack the door a bit and peek inside. Sitting on my couch, wearing what resembles a 1930s elevator operator's uniform, is Mickey, the mail boy of penis delivery fame. Why they make them wear these outfits, I have no idea. Maybe so we know who they are when we see them coming. Or maybe just to make them feel silly. Next to him on the couch is a white mailroom bucket bulging with cards and letters addressed to me. Mickey is poring over one of the letters and smiling, stupidly, completely unaware of my presence.

"Mickey, what do you think you're doing?"

Guiltily, and unsuccessfully, he attempts to shuffle the letter back into its envelope.

"Oh, sorry, Mr. S. I . . . I hope you don't mind."

"Why on earth are you reading my mail? Don't you know that's illegal?"

"Please don't turn me in." His voice trembles. "I can't help it, sir. I love to read, and with my paltry salary, I just can't afford books. This is the only way I can nourish my mind."

He looks up at me, and though his chin quivers and his pleading eyes begin to well up, I ain't buying it.

"You are so full of shit, Mickey. Why are you reading my letters?"

Dropping his pitiful pretense, he returns to his usual smarmy self. "Well, to be honest, Mr. S, I read everyone's letters. It's my little peccadillo. They make me feel like I'm not such a loser, after all."

"Good God, Mickey," I say, trying not to lean too hard on my disgust for him, "these are good-hearted, lovely people who have affection for the show and for me. That doesn't make them losers."

He holds up a letter for me to see. The words "I LOVE DATA!" have been scrawled next to a crude drawing of what I'm guessing is Data, surrounded by floating red hearts.

"Mickey, it's possible a child sent that!" I say, attempting to defend the never-to-be-Picasso.

"You think?" He slowly draws the letter under his nose, sniffing it as it drifts past, "and I suppose she doused it in L'Air du Temps before Mommy put her to bed?"

He's really pissing me off now. I know if I say what I'm thinking we'll wind up rolling around my trailer floor trading punches, and as puny as he is, he could probably still take me.

"Does Patrick know you read his letters?" I sputter.

I'm, of course, referring to Patrick Stewart, our captain and leader. As fine a man who ever commanded a starship. Or ever was in real life, for that matter. He does not suffer fools gladly.

"Sure he does. He caught me going through them and threatened to report me. But we made a little quid pro quo. He lets me read his mail, and in return, I lend him VHS copies of this year's Oscar contenders."

"What? You get Academy screeners? How?"

"Easy. I work in the mailroom. One of the studio execs, no names, is a member of the Academy. I swipe his tapes. He thinks they slipped up, forgot to send them, and he gets them to send more copies. I swipe those, too."

How many ways does this kid break the law? Wait a minute . . . could it be Mickey who sent me that putrid package? After all, he's the one who delivered it to my trailer. Nah, why would he waste his money on postage? He could've just put it in my trailer while I was filming. Unless he did that to throw me off the scent . . . Nah!

"Let me be clear about one thing, Mickey. When you go to prison, I won't be visiting."

He jumps up from the couch and, again, looks at me with those phony pleading eyes. "You're not going to cut me off, are you, Mr. S? Your letters are my favorites!"

Another thought occurs to me. "Mickey, what are Patrick's letters like?

"Oh, you know, typical stuff. Mainly, they just want an autographed photo of him in his Starfleet uniform. He gets a lot of mail, but I got to give him credit, he does his best to answer it all. Right now, he's only fourteen months behind."

"Yeah, but does he get, you know, threatening mail?"

"Oh, sure. I mean, nothing like yours. No body parts. Basically guys who want to beat him up because their wives are in love with him. *TV Guide*'s sexiest man in the galaxy, you know. Doesn't scare him, though. They train English actors in all sorts of self-defense."

I've had about as much as I can take for one night. "Get outta here, Mickey. I gotta take this makeup off. I need to go home and learn my lines for tomorrow."

"Yeah, I gotta get going myself. I hear a pepperoni lover's pizza calling my name." He heads for the door, then turns back to me. "I can offer you the same deal. You keep this between the two of us, let me read your letters, and I'll supply you with movies."

"Get out of here, Mickey!"

He tips his little monkey grinder hat, steps out of the trailer, and heads up the street. After a short beat, I lean out and call to him: "Hey! Do you have *Goodfellas*?"

He whirls around and replies, "What a great flick! It's gonna win Best Picture this year. I'd bet my life on it."

"Well, can I borrow it?"

"Sure, but Patrick's got it. Don't worry, you're next!" Flashing a Cagney-esque grin, he snaps both fingers and dances out of sight.

Having gotten as much of this makeup off as I can, I slip into my clothes, grab my stuff, and head for the door. The letter I caught Mickey reading is still open on the couch, half sticking out of its envelope. The pinkish stationery looks like something you would buy at a drugstore at Easter. Paper-clipped to the top is a Polaroid of a woman, early forties, with longish gravy-colored hair. Her smile seems forced and her eyes speak of a pain I hope I never find out about. Too late. I'm already reading.

> Hi, Brent,
>
> I have recently become a very big fan of yours. I love Data. You are so kind and have such a lovely voice. Also, you are very handsome. I watch your show every week and it brings me comfort and peace. I can hardly wait for the next episode.
>
> Shall I tell you a little about me?
>
> I am a Christian woman, married, with a three-year-old daughter. My husband is a traveling salesman. He has sold just about everything, but right now, it's dinettes. He is on the road most of the time driving all over Canada and the U.S. He seems to be home less and less these days. He works very hard. But I wish he wasn't gone so much. I am very lonely here, and sometimes I feel we hardly know each other anymore. We used to have a nice house when we lived in North Carolina. Now we live in a two-bedroom apartment in Canada. Long story.
>
> Well, that's all for now, I guess. You'll probably never see

this, but if you do, know that I think you are wonderful. I don't expect you to write me back. But if you did, I would be over the moon!

Respectfully,
Mrs. Loretta Gibson

I'm usually pretty removed when I read these things, but for some reason, this one kind of gets to me. Fuck you, Mickey.

SIX

UP ON THE ROOF

HOME. MY DOMICILE is a modest sixteen-hundred-square-foot Spanish in a neighborhood called Outpost Estates in the Hollywood Hills. This is the first time I've resided in a house since my mother was married to Sol. This sweet swank-ienda is my little piece of paradise after years of living on the third floor of a four-floor walk-up on the Upper West Side of Manhattan. It's quaint, quirky, and best of all, quiet. In New York City, the sound of footfalls coming from the apartment above me was a constant irritation.

Before jumping in the shower, I call for pizza delivery. There's a certain satisfaction I have in making this call. When I first arrived in Hollywood, I got a job delivering for Pizza Man, the late-night shift. In the "wee small hours of the morning," I transported pizza and chicken wings to night owls and weirdos. And occasionally to massage parlors. They were the most generous with tips. After about a dozen rings . . .

"Pizza Man, We Deliver. What can I get you?"

"Uh, yes, I'd like a large pepperoni lover's pizza and a side of pepperoni, please!"

Apparently, that little flimflam man, Mickey, got to me on more than one level.

"That's a large pepperoni lover's pizza and a side of pepperoni. Will that be all?"

"That's it."

"Your total is $12.50. Could I get your name, address, and phone number?"

After I give him the requested information, he promises to deliver my pie in thirty minutes or less.

Before he can hang up, I jump in. "Hey, can I ask you something? When you say thirty minutes or less, is that thirty minutes from when you picked up the phone or thirty minutes from when I ordered? Or is it thirty minutes from when you hang up? I'm trying to time a shower."

"Well, sir . . ."—a hint of irritation creeping into his voice—"Mr. . . . uh, Spiner . . . Wait a minute, are you the guy from *Star Trek*? Data?"

With some reluctance, and a touch of embarrassment, I give it up. "Yeah, that's, uh, that's me."

His tone alters dramatically. "Oh wow! I love your show! Great character, by the way!"

"Thanks, that's very kind."

"My favorite episode so far is the one where you created a child. What was it, 'The Offspring'?"

"Yeah . . . that's right. Uh, can I ask you another question? Is this part of the conversation included in the thirty minutes?"

"You'd better get in the shower now, Mr. Spiner. The delivery guy already left. Hell, if I'd known it was you, I'd have thrown in an order of garlic balls."

At warp speed, I jump in the shower and scrub what remains of Data out of my system. Slipping into my tattered terry-cloth robe, I settle down to learn a few lines before the Pizza Man deliveryperson arrives. Reaching into my backpack, I pull out what I assume is the script for this week's not particularly interesting episode. Instead, what I'm holding in my hand is the script of a far less interesting episode. The title on the cover reads *Ortiz and Data*. Below the title is the work number of the head of obsessives. Below that, in parentheses, he's jotted the words: *It could be Data and Ortiz, but I don't think that sounds as good.* This is the man to whom I am entrusting my life? Then it occurs to me that maybe I should give him a call and tell him about Todd. I mean, even though Ortiz is ridiculous, he is the law. On second thought, things could go terribly wrong, terribly quickly. Ortiz might overreact and arrest Todd on suspicion of stalking. Then the tabloids could get ahold of the information and print that I've lobbed accusations at a guest star. It could be very bad for both of us. His career could be damaged, all because of a baseless hunch. And even more important, I could come off like a jerk.

My eyelids are getting heavy. Today was long and unusually trying. If Pizza Man doesn't get here soon, I'm going to fall . . . *Zzzzzzzzzzzz.*

I'm driving down Park Avenue in New York City. The street is wet and shining, the way it looks after a recent shower. There's a meter attached to the dashboard with my license next to it. A photo of me looking very young. I'm driving a cab again. I don't know why I'm back doing that, but I don't have time to think about it. A doorman in front of one of those apartment buildings that mainly houses the old and wealthy flags me down. He opens the back door of the taxi. Out of nowhere, a young man wearing a white suit appears. As he turns to give the doorman a tip, I notice the back of his suit is covered in blood.

Great, *I think*, he's going to bleed all over my car.

He jumps in the back seat and says in a strangled voice, "Take me to the hospital."

"What's wrong with you?" I ask.

"My girlfriend stabbed me in the ass," he shouts. "Now go!"

I turn around to get a good look at him, and he shows me his bloody hand, which had been gripping his buttocks.

"Go! Now! Any hospital!" he screams in agony.

I gun the car forward, but suddenly it's like I've never driven these streets before. I'm completely lost. "Sir, if you could just tell me how to get there."

He pulls a large blade from out of nowhere and threatens me with it. "Go! Now!!!!"

"Please. Please don't hurt me!"

He takes the butt of the knife and repeatedly smashes it into the ceiling of the cab. THUNK.

"Go! Go!" he shrieks. THUNK . . . THUNK . . . THUNK.

I'm jolted awake to the sound of another thunk coming

from above me. Someone is walking on the roof of my quaint, quirky, quiet house in the hills. Still disoriented, I wonder if this is it. Is Lal here to castrate me? But why is she walking on the roof? Maybe all of this is a dream and I still live in New York? The fog begins to clear from my head as reality, or something resembling reality, finally comes into focus. Needing an equalizer, I vacillate between a kitchen knife and a limited-edition Joe DiMaggio–signed baseball bat. I go with the bat. I might accidentally fall on my knife.

Stealthily tiptoeing out to the front of the house, I look up and see a young man in his early twenties who, with great effort and no tools, is trying to dislodge a Saltillo tile from my roof. He doesn't notice that I'm looking right at him. A pizza box is balanced precariously on the ridge of the roof.

"Hey!" I shout.

He freezes, then slowly turns around to see me glaring at him. "Pizza Man, We Deliver," he says in a voice bordering on soprano.

"What?"

"We're required by the company to say that whenever we make a delivery."

I remember that particularly embarrassing greeting from my old Pizza Man days.

"What are you doing on my roof?" I demand, preparing to kiss his forehead with the sweet spot of my Louisville Slugger.

"Mr. Spiner . . . can I, uh, have a tile? It would mean a lot to me."

"A tile? No, you can't have a tile!" I yell back at him.

"Just one tile? And maybe you'll sign it? I could throw in an order of garlic balls."

Garlic balls are the crown jewel of Pizza Man, We Deliver. I consider it for a moment. "You have garlic balls?"

"Yes, sir, in the little oven in my car. They're somebody else's order, but if you let me have a tile they're yours."

"*No!*" I shout, coming to my senses. "I'm going inside and I'm calling your boss! When I come back out, you'd better be gone. And that pepperoni lover's pizza better be on my doorstep!"

Running back inside, I grab the cordless phone and dial Pizza Man, We Deliver. After twelve rings, I decide to take the phone with me and run back outside. Nearly tripping over the pizza box that is now on my doorstep, I look up to find the Pizza Man has gone. In his place is an empty spot where a tile used to be. The cordless is now on its seventeenth ring. Must be a busy night at Pizza Man, We Deliver. This is taking too much time. I'm exhausted and I have ten pages of technobabble to learn for tomorrow. Hanging up the phone, I pick up the pizza box and go back into the house. One truth becomes crystal clear in my mind. I should've called Domino's.

SEVEN   A BULLET FOR BRENT

A FEW DAYS later, entering my honeywagon after a long day of shooting, I find an envelope with a small bulge in the middle waiting for me on my desk. Something hard. The handwriting on the envelope—just my name, no return address—is disturbingly familiar. Inside is a letter along with something wrapped in a piece of paper. With shaking fingers, I lift it out of the envelope. Peeling off the wrapper, I'm confronted with another unwanted gift: a FUCKING BULLET! That old familiar roller coaster takes a steep dip down my gullet, where it meets what feels like billiard balls rolling around in my stomach. On closer examination, I notice writing on the wrapper. *My brother has your name on it.* I suck in a deep jagged breath. Petrified, I remove the letter and read it:

> *Dear Daddy,*
>
> *It has been so very hard not seeing you. I miss you. Don't you miss me? I picked out this bullet just for you. Do you*

like it? Does it feel like love when you hold it in your hand?

I'm very angry at you. You will know exactly how angry soon. Very soon, Daddy.

Your loving daughter,
Lal

I reach for the phone and dial the head of obsessives. Like Woody Woodpecker tapping on a tasty pine tree, my trembling hand jackhammers the phone against my ear.

Ring . . . ring . . . ring . . .

"C'mon, Ortiz!" I shout into the phone. Finally . . .

"Obsessives. Ortiz speaking," he answers, sounding oddly short of breath.

"Detective, this is Brent Spiner."

I wait for a response. Nothing but silence on the other end. "Detective, are you there?"

At last I hear his raspy voice. "Okay, fellas, that's all for today."

I can make out the sound of many footsteps leaving the room.

"Sorry, Mr. Spiner, I'm a little winded. I teach a yoga class to some of the boys on Wednesday afternoons. What's doing?"

"Detective, I got another letter from Lal. A very angry letter. And there was a bullet wrapped in a piece of paper, with the words *my brother has your name on it.*"

"Ooohhh, that is disturbing. It means Lal has another bullet that's meant for you."

"Yes, it's disturbing! It's FUCKING TERRIFYING! Jesus, why is this happening to me?"

"Let me give you a metaphor . . ."

"No, please don't! Just help me. Tell me what to do."

It occurs to me that asking advice from a possibly insane detective/masseur/yoga instructor is a fool's game. Nonetheless, I push ahead. "Detective, I'm starting to lose it."

"Yes, I can tell that from the sound of your voice. Very tense. What would you think about coming to the yoga class on Wednesdays?"

I really don't know how to answer that. Thankfully, he doesn't press the matter.

"Oh, hey, I almost forgot," he says excitedly. "I've got big news for you. We ran the fingerprints on that letter you brought in. The prints don't match anyone in our database, so it's not a known perp. Hey, I never thought of that. DATA base! Get it?" He laughs idiotically, as if I could possibly find humor in that.

Stop the world, I want to get off. Or at least stop him.

"Listen, Mr. Spiner, I'm no psychiatrist, but I don't think you should be alone tonight. You sound a little shaky. Look, some of the fellows here at the precinct are doing a reading of my script this evening. Would you want to come? Maybe you could play yourself? . . . I mean Data? I'm sure it would be a real thrill for the guys, not to mention for me."

Uncharacteristically, this lunatic is finally right about something. It's company that I need, and I don't mean his cast of thespians in blue. No, I need to be with someone who might comfort me in my near hysteria.

My mind immediately goes to Mandy. Sure, Mandy. Sweet Mandy. Mandy is an actress . . . of sorts. She's been working in the business since she was a child. You can spot her in the background of movies like *Bugsy Malone* and a couple of late Tony Curtis pictures. Her adult roles haven't gotten much better. Though drop-dead gorgeous, she's monolithically untalented. We went on a few dates which I thought went pretty well—fun conversation, lots of laughs, first base, second base, third base . . . Then she met somebody else and unceremoniously dumped me. She wouldn't tell me who he was. All she revealed was that his father was one of the Rolling Stones. I was devastated. I didn't really give a damn if it was Keith Richards's or Charlie Watts's kid, but a gnawing in my gut told me it was probably Mick's progeny. And I definitely get no satisfaction from that. A few months later I heard their affair had fizzled out. I was relieved, but I didn't call her. She had treated me like shit, and besides, I never actually thought we were right for each other. The hell with her.

But now, suddenly, I want to be there again. Inside her little cottage in the hills with the blinds drawn, in the arms of Mandy. Safe Mandy. Comforting Mandy. Beautiful Mandy. Blue-eyed Mandy, great-smelling Mandy, two-timing Mandy. Okay, okay, in this time of existential horror, I'm willing to overlook a few things. I dial her number.

"Hello?"

My heart leaps into my throat as I hear her voice for the first time in months. A decibel or two north of Betty Boop, but I don't care, I need her. I answer tentatively . . .

"Hi, Mandy, it's . . . it's Brent."

"Brent! Well, hi, stranger!"

In my mind, I laugh and cry at the same time. Love-lust instantly pulling me away from the fear of Lal shooting me in the face. Mandy . . . sweet, self-absorbed Mandy. God, I've missed her.

"I've been thinking a lot about you lately . . . I hope you don't mind that I called."

"No, of course not! I've been thinking about you, too."

"Really? You have?" I say, trying not to sound too needy.

"Yeah. What are you up to? Are you on set?"

"Just wrapped. Uh . . . are you . . . busy?"

"Not at all. I'm whipping up a plate of prima pasta vera. Are you hungry?"

I'm even willing to overlook the fact that she called *pasta primavera* prima pasta vera.

"So hungry," I respond ravenously.

"Well, c'mon over, silly."

Minutes later I'm driving to Mandy's place, my car filled with the aroma of Pinaud Lilac Vegetal. That's the stuff the barber used to put on the back of my neck when I was a kid. Been splashing it on my face since I started shaving. Cheap aftershave, but it has an intoxicating scent. At least I hope it does. I can't remember the last time I had sex. But oddly, as I head toward what I hope will be the end of a serious dry spell, I find myself reflecting on my first experience with carnal knowledge. Maybe it's the Lilac Vegetal triggering the memory of that fateful night. My older brother, Ronnie, chaperoned me to a spot in Houston called the Blue Top Courts, where every guy in my high school lost his virginity. It was always on a Saturday night, and we returned to school the next Monday, fooling ourselves into believing we were no longer boys, but mature men. It was a ritual. I can't imagine that sort of foolishness happening today, but twenty-five years ago, that's what the guys I grew up with did. The group of run-down bungalows was located on Telephone Road, on the other side of the tracks. There weren't actually any tracks—that's just what they say about places like that. It was an unusually frigid and blustery evening when Jesse, the pimp, showed me to bungalow 11, then left me at the door with these words:

"Little Tinker Toy will show you what to do."

"Little Tinker Toy." I liked the sound of that. I knocked on the door, and a lilting voice on the other side bade me enter. When I walked in, I saw her sitting up on the bed, and if memory serves me, looking back, she bore an uncanny resemblance to Ed McMahon. I started to shiver. I don't know if it was because I was scared or cold, or because she looked like Johnny Carson's second banana in a nightgown. I didn't think I could do it. But I didn't want to hurt her feelings. She seemed like a nice person. So I decided to blame it on my youth. "I'm so sorry, Tinker Toy, but I've never done this before, and I . . ."

"Don't be shy, child," she interrupted, patting the side of the bed. "Take off your clothes and come sit here."

Having no will of my own, I of course obliged. I stripped down to my boxers, walked over, and timidly sat on the edge of the bed. She took me by the shoulders, gently turned me toward her, and then pinned me to the pillow. She was so strong. So wise. She looked me right in the eyes and said, "Kid, if you've got ten dollars, I've got the keys to the kingdom of heaven."

So I bravely got up, removed a ten-spot from my jeans, placed it on the dresser, and returned to her bed. And then we made mad, beautiful . . . something. Cost me about a buck a second. Jesse was right, she knew her business. Since I had the rest of my bar mitzvah money in my pocket, I went another couple of rounds in the Tinker Toy School of Love. She was amazing. All in all, I was in and out the door in fifteen minutes, but the memory has lasted the rest of my life.

I slip Sinatra's *It Might As Well Be Swing* into the CD player and the chairman wails for an unnamed woman to fly him from the Earth to the Moon and then on to other planets. To let him see what spring is like on Jupiter and Mars! All while holding hands, kissing, worshiping, adoring. As I pull up in front of Mandy's house, Frank ends the song with the ever-familiar "I . . . LOVE . . . YOU!!!!!!!"

EIGHT   HELLO, MY LOVELY

WHEN SHE OPENS the door, I nearly faint. She is even more gorgeous than I remembered. We hold each other tightly and I no longer care about her betrayal. Or the fact that she is at least a head taller than me. Or anything else for that matter. We kiss tenderly and at that moment I can think of no other place in the universe I'd rather be. Not Jupiter or Mars or even the god-damn Moon. We have a wonderful dinner, and afterwards, she excuses herself briefly and goes into the bathroom, giving me the opportunity to shake a few drops of Binaca on my tongue. Whoo. When she returns, we adjourn to the couch. I put my arm around her and she rests her head on my shoulder. Feeling oddly connected to her, I want to know more about her.

"Mandy, tell me a secret. Something I don't know about you. Something intimate."

"Hmm, let me think . . . Okay, before I met you, I dated James Woods for a few months. He broke it off when he found out I was over eighteen."

49

James Woods? I was horrified! I tried not to show it, but I was utterly sickened by this new wrinkle. Who is this woman with her head on my shoulder? How could she have such disgusting taste in men?

"Now it's your turn," she purred. "Tell me a secret you've never told anyone else."

Until the pig's penis showed up at my door, my life had been pretty normal, so I rack my brain to come up with something. Then I remembered . . .

"Well, I was a virgin till I was sixteen. My older brother took me to a prostitute. The first woman I ever had sex with was a dead ringer for Ed McMahon."

Mandy was as appalled by this as I was by her James Woods revelation. "Oh my God! You poor thing. You could've been scarred for life."

"Yeah, I know. Luckily I wasn't. Except that since then, every time I watch *The Tonight Show,* I get an erection."

Her head left my shoulder as she sat bolt upright and scooched a few inches away, the look on her face reminding me that gorgeous and vacant could exist simultaneously.

"That was a joke. I was just kidding."

"I know," she says unconvincingly.

Hoping to get back up to where we were, I slide over and try to kiss her, but she stops me with a hand to the chest.

"Are you okay?" she asks with genuine concern. "I didn't want to say anything over dinner, but you seem kind of stressed out. There's something . . . I don't know, something different about you."

Clearly, there was an elephant in the room. A pachyderm named Lal. I was hoping I could hide my fear from Mandy. I didn't want her to get sucked into my nightmare. Not yet. Not while she seemed so pleased to be with me again.

"Mandy, I don't want to spoil things. And I don't want to make my problems your problems."

She takes my hand in hers and presses it against her breasts. I'd never noticed before that her eyes cross slightly when she gets serious. It's actually kind of cute.

"It's okay, darling. We're getting to know each other again. I want to help. I want to be here for you. Can't you tell me what it is?"

She seems different, too. So sensitive. My God, she called me darling. I want to confide in her. I want to tell her everything. And so I do. I tell her about the pig's penis and Lal and the letters and the blood and the bullet. Everything.

She wraps me in her arms and lovingly strokes my back. "Oh, my poor baby. I'm so sorry this is happening to you."

She holds me even tighter and plants tiny butterfly kisses on my neck. This is all moving so quickly. With each kiss, my terror subsides. I return the favor. Such a lovely swanlike neck. At last our mouths meet in perfect harmony, as if they were designed for each other. Absolute bliss. And as our lips part, she utters four words that will forever define her for me.

"You have to go."

"Wh . . . What?" I say, confused, as if abruptly woken from a glorious Technicolor dream.

"You're putting me in danger, Brent. While we were eating

and laughing and drinking wine, this Lal person could have shot us both through the window! I like you, Brent, but not enough to die for. I need you to leave. Now."

Ashamed and a little guilty, I offer a feeble apology. "I'm sorry, Mandy. You're right. I shouldn't have come here."

She takes me by the hand and leads me to another part of her house. I was still hoping for sex, but since we arrive in her laundry room, I figure that's off the table. The overwhelming fear creeps back into my soul as she points to a small window above her washer-dryer.

"That leads to an alley behind the house," she says. "It's dark out there, and no one will see you till you get to your car. You should be able to squeeze through if you suck your stomach in. And please take off your shoes so you don't scratch the appliances."

I do as she asks, but before dropping from the window to the pavement outside, I take one last look at her. "Can I see you again sometime?" I inquire pitifully.

"Of course, darling. If you're still alive in a couple of months, maybe we can take in a movie?"

I make it back to my car, unscathed. For now. I drive into the night, listening to Sinatra again.

"You're like a falling star that dies / and seems to go on dying, when no one cares . . ."

Frank understands.

NINE   THE ANDROID ONLY RINGS ONCE

TEN O'CLOCK. I drive past Pink's Hot Dogs on La Brea. God, I could use a chili dog. Mandy's prima pasta vera was delicious, but it wasn't filling. Wait, what am I thinking? I can't stop. What if Lal is following me? Plus, the current state of my stomach could never digest those puppies. Besides, is it actually food I crave? No, what I really need is a friend. I continue south onto the 101 Highway and head for Tarzana, once the multi-acre estate of the great Edgar Rice Burroughs. Now, tucked away on a small parcel of that great land sits the home of my pal Commander Riker, Jonathan Frakes. He shares this domicile with his bride, the beautiful Genie Francis, an icon in her own right from the celebrated daytime drama *General Hospital*. When I was a young actor in New York, I always arranged my auditions so I could be home in time to catch her show. As was true of the rest of America, my day was not complete without the trials of Luke and Laura. But now it was Jonathan and Genie I needed. Frakes and Francis. What a couple. Like the

Tracy and Hepburn of the San Fernando Valley. Genie will be warm and understanding. And Jonathan, well, Jonathan is big.

Taking the Reseda Boulevard exit, I pull over when I spot a pay phone on the corner of a strip mall. My Dodger cap pulled low over my head, I flip the collar of my windbreaker and fasten it tight around my throat. It's a chilly night. You know, 65 degrees, Los Angeles kind of chilly. Slinking stealthily into the booth, I slide the door shut. The light above me goes black, making the ambience more than a little surreal. With trembling fingers, I manage to drop a quarter into the slot, dial their number, and pray that someone is home.

"Frakes residence!" booms a welcome baritone voice.

"Johnny, it's Brent," I say in a voice so hushed even I can barely hear it.

"Sorry, who is this? I couldn't quite get th—"

"It's Brent!"

"Oh, hey, man, what's up?"

"Uh, can I come over?" I say, struggling not to sound too pathetic.

"Now?" he asks with genuine curiosity.

I don't typically drop in late at night when we're working the next day. In fact, I never drop in.

"Right now!" I say, losing the battle.

"Where are you?"

"Yeah, um, I'm at a pay phone on the corner of Reseda Boulevard. It's kind of dark. But it's . . . you know, relatively clean, so I guess there are people that keep it—"

"Come over right now," he says, interrupting my irrational blather.

Five minutes later I arrive at Jonathan and Genie's place and park a few houses down. I walk quickly, then run the last few steps, looking behind me even as I press the bell. The door opens and Genie appears like the Angel of Mercy.

"Hi!" she says, beaming her glowing Pepsodent smile. "Are you okay?"

Wrapping her arm in mine, she guides me inside, a look of deep concern on her face. Clearly, Jonathan has appraised her of my unusual behavior.

"Hi, Genie," I say, smiling back, a pained look on my face. "Do you mind if we close the drapes? Also, I could really use a . . ."

His ESP on full alert, Jonathan appears with a glass of whiskey. As Genie pulls the drapes, I slug down the shot of Chivas. Normally, that would burn going down, but because my adrenaline is pumping, it's more like a soothing spoonful of honey.

"To your health, my friend. Now what the hell is going on?" Jonathan asks.

"Guys, I'm being stalked. She—or he—wants me dead. This is serious."

They glance at each other surreptitiously. I can see the questions running through their minds. Is this real? Has he gone completely screwy?

I tell them about the pig penis, the Lal letters, the head of obsessives, the bullet, and most recently, Mandy kicking me out of her house.

"And it looked like it might work out this time. We were really connecting for a change, and—"

"Let's be honest," Jonathan says, cutting me off. "You're the one who always said you weren't right for each other."

"That's true," I admit. "I mean, she says prima pasta vera, for God's sake! Who says that?"

Her eyes filled with empathy, Genie gently takes my hand.

"Oh, Brent, have you been sleeping at all?

"Not much. I'm becoming a basket case, and that's so not like me. Could I get another drink?"

Jonathan, already two steps ahead of me, hands me another scotch.

"Well, what about this guy, the head of obsessives—what is he doing?" he asks.

"Nothing. He says he has no leads."

"You should stay here tonight," Genie offers. "Stay in our guest room. You're in no shape to go home."

"But what if Lal followed me? I don't want to put you guys in danger."

Jonathan jumps in decisively. I can see in an instant why he was cast as Riker, Picard's number one.

"We have a state-of-the-art security system. No one is getting on our property, I promise you."

"Well, okay, but you should know that lately I tend to scream in my sleep," I admit.

"No problem," Johnny assures me, "you can sleep in the

guesthouse. It's soundproof and has the same security system as in here. Feel free to scream your lungs out."

The combined effects of alcohol and exhaustion are slamming me simultaneously. "I think I need to lie down."

Jonathan throws an arm around my shoulders, and together they escort me, on unsteady legs, to my night's sanctuary.

"I'll take my clothes off in the morning," I say nonsensically, and plop myself onto the bed.

"Whatever you want," says Jonathan as Genie tucks me in.

Looking up at the natural beauty of Genie and the annoying handsomeness of Frakes, I feel a warm glow inside, right where the billiard balls usually are. It's such a gift to be taken care of by wise, attractive people when someone wants to kill you.

"You're such good friends," I sputter, tears stinging my eyes. "I'm so embarrassed."

"Don't be embarrassed. Let it go. Usually you struggle with expressing real human emotions," says Jonathan.

"Oh, yeah, me and Data. Two androids in a pod," I mumble as my vision begins to blur.

"It's going to be okay, Brent. Try to get some sleep," Genie says, stroking my hair the way one would comfort a child.

As they tiptoe to the door, Jonathan offers one final instruction before turning out the lights. "I'm going to set the alarm. Your call time tomorrow is earlier than mine, so before you leave, shut it off. The code is 1701D. Sleep well. We're here if you need us."

1701D. Ha, that's cute. The call letters of the starship *Enterprise* on our show. 'Course, if I was a killer, that might be the first thing I'd think of. The ambient light from the moon shining through the window is foggy. Again, the camera lens with Vaseline smeared over it. The dark tunnel begins to close around me until everything goes black.

Cruising the streets of Los Angeles. I'm in the passenger seat. Ortiz is at the wheel.

"Well, Data, I think I've got a lead on this guy. If we catch him, it could mean a big promotion for both of us. Hey, we could both wind up Full Commanders!"

He laughs like an idiot, but I don't care. I'm too focused on my hands. They are gold.

"This douchebag has been responsible for the unhappiness of a lot of people," he says as he spits a lungful out the driver's side window.

He doesn't seem to care that the window is closed. As the thick glob slides down the glass, I find myself thinking how uncouth this is. And how unusual. I mean, his office was so tidy.

"How many people has he killed?" I inquire.

"He hasn't exactly killed anyone. He just murders their spirits. Makes them withdraw, hide their feelings inside. Poor saps are never fully themselves again."

There is something frightening, and at the same time, familiar about all this.

"Is he that powerful? How does he do that?"

Ortiz turns to face me. His eyes narrow as he shouts a few decibels more than necessary. "WITH FEAR!!!"

His eyes shift as he spots something and makes a sharp turn down an unlit alley. "That's him!" he shouts.

At the end of the street, a man, maybe a homeless person, warms his hands over a trash-can bonfire.

"I'll get him. You stay here. If he runs, call for backup."

"You got it," I respond confidently. Though to be honest, I'm not exactly sure how to call for backup. Do I have that number?

Ortiz grabs the man and spins him around. With superhuman strength he tosses him onto the top of the hood, pressing his face against the windshield. The man's face, though distorted, is oddly handsome. He looks up at me, staring directly into my eyes. Dear God, it's my stepfather!!!

I wake with a start, hyperventilating, momentarily confused about my whereabouts. Oh yeah, Jonathan's guest house. Check my Timex. Five A.M. If I step on it, I can make it to work on time. Good thing I didn't take my clothes off. Hopping out of bed, I punch in the code on the alarm: 1701D. I run to my car and slide behind the wheel. As I look ahead, through the windshield, vague images come into my mind. Driving into the early morning darkness, I struggle to remember, but typically, only snippets of my dream remain.

These 5:45 A.M. call times suck, but at least there's no traffic. The general mental discomfort that envelops me is now coupled with the awful realization that I didn't learn my lines last night. My dialogue is always impossible, a plethora of technobabble that would challenge even the best of memories. Plus, it's difficult to get the words out of your mouth. You basically have to train your mouth muscles to wrap themselves around words they've never spoken before. My usual deal with myself

is that I can't go to sleep until I can say the next day's work out loud, perfectly. Fortunately, I have a pretty good memory. Except last night I forgot. I'd love to be more like LeVar, who can look at this word salad a couple of times and then nail it on the first take.

Stepping into my trailer, I see that Mickey has left a small stack of mail on my couch. The top letter is adorned with a couple of Canadian stamps and the familiar address of one Mrs. Loretta Gibson. Against my better instincts, I read it.

> *Dear Brent,*
>
> *I can't believe you called me last night! I was afraid I'd never hear from you again, but I never expected a phone call! I'm soooo happy! The things you said! You're so naughty! Oh my goodness, it puts thoughts in my head! I can't believe you feel that way about me; that you want to do those things with me! I shouldn't say this, but I feel the same way about you. And I want you to do all of those things to me. I hope, if we are ever together, that I don't disappoint you. Even though I have a child, I'm not really very experienced in those ways. My husband and I don't have sexual relations very often. And to be honest, I don't really feel that way about him anymore. I haven't for some time. But I am still a healthy woman and I have needs. I know you could teach me things I've never dreamed of. You already have.*
>
> *Please keep calling me. Andrew comes home tomorrow, but only for a week. Call me after the 20th. And, please*

don't be afraid to say it is you. I hope God doesn't punish
me for saying this. But I want to know you better. In every
way. Wink wink.

Yours,
Loretta

Is it possible that Loretta might be Lal? Or is she just an unfulfilled housewife, desperate for affection? Or is she completely insane? Did anyone actually call her? Browsing the other letters in the stack, I find them to be typical fan mail. Sweet and supportive and in need of an autographed picture. The kind of letters I've dreamed of getting since I became an actor. And for a brief moment, I'm happy to be alive.

TEN

THE FBI CALLS

HAVING BEEN PROPERLY gilded by the great Mr. West-more, I return to my trailer to get into costume. As I'm about to zip up my space suit, the phone rings.

"Hello?"

"Brent Spiner, please."

"Speaking."

"Mr. Spiner, this is Agent Cindy Lou Jones. I'm an investigator with the FBI."

"FBI?!"

"I'd like to stop by the set today and ask you a few questions."

The woman speaking on the phone has a husky, sexy voice, like from a 1940s film noir. Think Veronica Lake. You wouldn't expect that from an FBI agent. At least I wouldn't.

"Yes, sure, but why?"

"I'll explain when I get there. Here's my office phone number, just in case. I know things on a set can get delayed, people get sent home, things go long."

I write down the number, say goodbye, and hang up. She seems to know a lot about how things go on a film set. And then I wonder if the person who just called me is a real FBI agent? Or was it Lal? As usually happens when I get nervous, the roller coaster heads to my stomach again. Maybe I have acid reflux? I should probably see a gastroenterologist. I dial the number she gave me, hoping it's legit.

"Federal Bureau of Investigation. How may I direct your call?"

"Agent Jones, please."

"We have fourteen agents named Jones. Which one do you want?"

"Oh, sorry. Do you have a Cindy Lou Jones?"

"Please hold."

Within moments, Cindy Lou answers. "Agent Jones speaking."

"Hi, Agent Jones. This is Brent Spiner. I hate to bother you, but I just wanted to make sure you're, well, you."

I can almost hear her smile. "No problem, Mr. Spiner, I understand completely. In fact, it's very wise of you to check me out."

She understands me! She thinks I'm wise. She oughta know, she's FBI. And that voice.

✳

A few hours later I'm sitting, sans makeup, at a conference room table in our production offices. I've been told to be there alone for my first meeting with the FBI. The door opens and a young woman, in what I would guess to be her early thirties, immaculate in a drab women's business suit, strides into the room. Call me crazy, but she's a dead ringer for Jodie Foster in *Silence of the Lambs*. Dirty blond bob, fantastic blue eyes, even that little ski-slope nose. She smiles professionally and extends her hand, and I take it. I haven't felt a grip that firm since, well, since my stepfather's.

"Mr. Spiner, Cindy Lou Jones. A pleasure to meet you. I enjoy your work. I'm a big fan of the show."

Good Lord, does everybody watch this show? We're syndicated and our ratings aren't really that great.

"Thanks. I presume Data is your favorite character?" I ask flirtatiously.

"Actually, I'm more of a Captain Picard kind of gal."

"Ah, well, he is amazing," I reply, trying to cloak my disappointment.

Pleasantries over, she gets down to business. "The reason I'm here is because a letter addressed to you had a razor blade in it. This blade cut the hand of a U.S. postal worker downtown. Not good. That automatically triggers a federal investigation. Nobody screws with the U.S. postal service."

Cindy Lou removes an envelope from her satchel. It has dried blood on it, near the carefully handwritten name BRENT SPINER. Inside is a razor blade.

"This was inside as well," she says, handing me a folded piece of stationery.

I unfold it to reveal a correspondence written in an extremely disturbing fashion. Each letter of a word was cut from a different source, a magazine or a book. Various colors and sizes pasted clumsily together to spell out the text. You've seen this in the movies.

> *Dear Daddy,*
>
> *Something terrible happened to me. Now it's your turn. I want the pain to stop. I love you to death.*
>
> *Lal*

I look up at Cindy Lou. No change of expression. She's seen it all before.

"Will you please help me?" I whisper pathetically.

She places her hand on my shoulder. It feels instantly comforting, like I've known her for years. "Don't worry, Mr. Spiner, we'll find this person. That's what we do. Lal was the name of your daughter in 'The Offspring,' wasn't it?"

"Well, Data's daughter, technically."

"Of course. Great episode, by the way. Can you tell me anything else that would be helpful?"

I tell her about the pig's penis floating in blood and the first letter I left with Ortiz, and Todd, the guest star, and even Loretta. I give her the most recent Lal letter and the bullet that came with it. Cindy Lou compares the envelopes.

"Same handwriting. But no return addresses. And postmarked from different cities. Curious. I'll take these letters and the bullet for fingerprint analysis. Let me have one of the letters from this Loretta person, too. We're using a new tool called DNA analysis that might give us some answers. I'd also like to talk to your coworkers, see if they can shed some light on who this person is. Is that possible?"

Twenty minutes later, the regular cast members join us in the conference room. Everyone except Wil Wheaton, of course, who is much too young to be a part of this. Agent Jones tells them that the FBI is opening an investigation into a serious matter concerning my safety. She briefly describes the pertinent details and asks if anyone has any relevant information that might be helpful. The room grows silent as my friends take in this information with varying degrees of shock and dismay.

Finally, LeVar breaks the tension. "I knew that pig's penis was bad mojo. Speaking of pig, anyone want to go for barbecue after we wrap?"

As a few hands go up, Jonathan interrupts. "I guess I should have mentioned this, but Genie received a letter from this Lal person. It was sent to her on her set at ABC."

"What? Jesus Christ, Johnny, why didn't you say something last night?" I ask.

"I'm sorry, Brento. We didn't really think much of it. Just a stupid letter from some nut. Then when you told us about the Lal letters, it suddenly made sense. But you were in such bad shape last night, we didn't want to upset you even more."

"Do you still have that letter, Mr. Frakes?" Agent Jones asks.

"Yeah, actually I've got it right here."

Jonathan reaches into his man bag. Very few men are man

enough to pull off a man bag, but then, very few men are Jonathan Frakes. Jonathan produces an envelope and hands it to Cindy Lou. She examines it carefully.

"Looks to be the same handwriting," she says, removing the letter and reading it aloud in that killer voice. "'Dear Genie Francis. You don't know me, but I know you. And I know what your husband has been doing with my daddy. Did you know they were perverts? Make him stop. Or I will. Your friend, Lal.'"

She looks at Jonathan and asks, "Mr. Frakes, does any of this mean anything to you?"

Jonathan thinks for a moment. "Not really. I mean, Brent is cute, but he's really not my type," he replies with a wink.

The room laughs nervously, the tension momentarily relieved.

"Have any of the rest of you received anything like this?" she asks.

The others all shake their heads no.

"Well, please keep an eye out. This person could easily focus on any one of you. Should you receive anything strange or hear anything possibly related to this, please inform me—and Mr. Spiner—immediately."

She turns to Patrick and drops her professional demeanor, becoming more of a federal government fangirl. "If it wouldn't be too much trouble, Mr. Stewart, could I possibly get an autograph? I've been a huge fan since I saw you in *I, Claudius* on PBS."

She holds out a piece of paper and a pen and Patrick signs

it with his usual flourish. Though I feel a wave of jealousy wash over me, a part of me is also intrigued. She watches PBS. And hell, I couldn't even make it through *I, Claudius.*

Cindy Lou carefully puts the autograph in a folder and then passes out her FBI business cards.

"I'll be in touch, Mr. Spiner. Don't hesitate to call if you need me."

"I will. And thank you so much for your help, Agent Jones."

She slings her bag over her shoulder and makes her exit. Gazing out the window as she strides down the pathway and out of sight, I feel a sense of relief that the FBI is now involved. And even more so, that Cindy Lou Jones is on my case.

My friends gather around me, each offering their full support and encouragement before heading back to set. As everyone leaves, Patrick takes me aside.

"Brent, a moment, if you will. I know this sounds morbid, but I've actually wondered to myself which one of us would be the first to be stalked by some crazy person. Frankly, you were the last one on my list. I was sure it would be me. Or at the very least, Jonathan."

"Well, some people find me irresistible," I shoot back, slightly offended.

"Oh, of course you are, dear boy," he says without much conviction. "I'm appalled over these threats to your life. It's all quite sick, and at the same time intriguing. You know, I've always been fascinated with the mysteries of the human psyche. I assumed that since my character is, of course, the Captain, the leader, it was more likely that some wildly unstable person would become fixated on me, my passion, my years with the Royal Shakespeare Company."

"I know I would be," I say, getting a grip on my dignity.

"Well, whoever it is, that story line about you creating a daughter seems to have triggered deep hostility toward you. She or he keeps addressing you as Daddy."

"Yeah, it's extremely creepy. Jesus, Patrick, I feel like I'm a character in some insane piece of fan fiction."

"And yet, ironically, it is we who created the world this person's imagination is currently inhabiting. We opened the door, and he or she walked right in. With all the psychodrama happening on the show, I'm surprised this doesn't occur more often. We should caution the writers to consider this going forward."

I think about all the story lines on the show—wild, emotional, personal, tragic, intense—and all the story lines to come. Are there more would-be stalkers out there formulating bizarre relationships with our characters? Have we opened Pandora's box? Roddenberry's box?

"One last thing," he offers. "As you may or may not know, we were schooled at the RSC in a wide variety of martial arts and fighting techniques. I want you to know, I'm here for you."

Humbled and touched, I wrap my arms around him. "God, Patrick, it means the world to me that you'd be willing to defend me."

"No, no, don't get me wrong. I'm not suggesting throwing myself in harm's way. I'm offering to teach you some of my self-defense skills. Give a man a fish and . . ." His voice trails off. "Well, you know that saying. Buck up, old man, it'll all be fine."

He claps me on the shoulder and marches off to once again save the universe.

I hike back to my trailer to grab my things when Gates Mc-Fadden pops her head in. Gates plays the ship's doctor on the show, Dr. Crusher. We first met years ago in New York City when I was acting in a play produced by her boyfriend. At the time, I found her to be extremely bright, and clearly, quite stunning. Nothing's changed.

"Hey, thought you might need a drink. Want to join us? We're headed over to Lucy's for a margarita."

"Boy, I could really use . . ." I say, walking toward her, when I'm suddenly stopped dead in my tracks. Over her shoulder, I spy the figure of none other than Todd, our guest star.

"You know Todd, right?" Gates asks.

"Uh . . . well, we didn't have any scenes together, but yeah, we've spoken. Hi Todd," I stammer.

"I've known Todd for years. He and his wife met in my eighteenth-century clowning class when I was teaching at NYU."

"Brent, I uh . . . I have a confession to make," Todd injects. Here it comes.

"Because I was so disappointed that I didn't get the role of Data, I never watched the show. Gates has been giving me shit for it. But since I got this gig, I borrowed her tapes and I've been watching the whole first season. I gotta tell you, you're fantastic. I could never have done what you have. You own this part."

"Oh, well, thanks. That's very kind of you," I say, beginning to feel foolish. I don't know, maybe I was wrong about Todd. Maybe I was projecting?

"Can I brag about you?" Gates asks of Todd.

"Oh, Gates, no, don't," he says, attempting to stop her.

"Todd organized a program at the motion picture retirement home. Once a week, he and a bunch of actors do play readings for the folks who live there. Really cheers them up. He's gotten some big names to join him, too."

Oh my God, this guy is a saint. And I'm an idiot.

"Come on. Come grab a drink with us," Gates says. "It'll help take your mind off things."

"Thanks, but I . . . I'm kind of beat. I think I'm just going to go home and turn in," I offer weakly.

"Okay, Brento, sleep well. And maybe carry a big stick." She smiles encouragingly. "If you change your mind, we're right across the street."

They start to walk away, but I can't, in good conscience, leave it like this.

"Hey, Todd!" I call out. "Hope we get to work together next time. Maybe I can join your group sometime?"

He shoots me a thumbs-up as they round the corner by Stage 8.

Well, that's one suspect off the list. A friend of Gates's from her eighteenth-century clowning class, of all things. I couldn't feel stupider. There's only one clown here. A twentieth-century clown. Me.

Grabbing my backpack off the couch, I spot something unwanted. Underneath it is a letter with my name spelled out in very familiar handwriting. Curiosity gets the best of me and I open it.

Dear Daddy,

You know what I like about razor blades? They're so small! You can hide them just about anywhere. In your mouth, in the palm of your hand, even in your shoe!

Do you like razor blades? I know you sometimes get a straight-razor shave at that barber on Melrose after you soak at the Beverly Hot Springs. Think of me the next time you're there. At the barber's, I mean. Maybe I could give you a shave someday. Nice and close.

Your loving daughter,
Lal

A few beads of red dot the page. Blood. Someone's blood.

ELEVEN   STRANGERS ON A STARSHIP

PARKING MY CAR a block away from my house, I climb over my next-door neighbor's fence, sneak quietly across his lawn, and vault over the fence separating our property into my backyard. I'm not taking any chances. Entering silently through the back door, trying not to breathe, I stand frozen, listening for unwanted sounds. Nothing. Without turning on any lights, I make sure the doors are locked and bolted. I feel my way to my bathroom and strip down to my chosen sleeping attire, my Calvin Klein gray briefs. Somehow I manage to find my toothbrush and the toothpaste and quickly scrub my teeth. From the sound of things, I also hit the toilet perfectly with my final evening's pee. Maybe I'll find out differently in the morning. Then the phone rings. I'm not answering. Let the machine pick up. My outgoing message plays.

"Hi, this is Brent. I'm not home right now, but if you'll leave your name and number, I'll call you back as soon as I can." Beep!

There is an uncomfortable pause while I wait for someone to leave a message. Finally a man clears his throat. Someone speaks hesitantly in an unfamiliar voice. "Mr. Spiner, you don't know me, but I work at the Franklin Kurtz Mental Health Facility for Children in Duluth, Minnesota. I . . . I know about the letters you've been getting. If you want to know more, you should speak to the director of psychiatry here. Her name is Dr. Sandra Ogilvy. That's all I can tell you."

The line goes dead. A chill goes through me as I grope my way to my phone machine. I play the man's message again. The Franklin Kurtz Mental Health Facility for Children. Holy shit! What the hell is going on here?

Slipping into the feathers, I pull the covers up over my head. If it turns out someone is coming to kill me tonight, I don't want to see it. I just want sleep. Safe, refreshing sleep. "To sleep, perchance to dream." So tired. Fear is exhausting. The last remaining light in my waking mind fades to black.

I'm in costume and makeup as Data on the Enterprise *Bridge set. We're about to shoot an important scene.*

Rick Berman, our executive producer, appears and makes an announcement. "I have some exciting news. There's been a last-minute change in casting. The role of Captain Picard will now be played by Brent's stepfather, Sol."

Light applause as everyone accepts this as completely normal and takes their places.

"Quiet, everyone! And . . . action!" the director yells.

A Louis Prima song blasts over speakers. It seems odd and out of place till I remember that Sol used to play his records while we ate dinner. The turbolift doors to the Bridge open and Sol dances in, wearing an immaculate Starfleet captain's uniform. He's young, the same age as when he lived with my mother, brother, and me. He does a few well-executed moves, surveys his crew, sees me, and smiles. I can't tell if he's happy to see me, but I know I'm not particularly thrilled to see him.

"Commander Data, it's been such a long time."

"Yes, it has," I say, the fear rising in my loins. Assuming I have loins.

"What did you say to me?" he replied angrily. "Didn't I always tell you to address an adult as SIR?"

"I'm sorry, Sol. But I am an adult. I mean, Captain. I mean, sir."

His nostrils flare as he glares at me.

"Uh, what should I say if I'm talking to a female?" I ask, hoping to get under his skin as I always did.

"Don't get cute with me, Commander," he barks as he turns and points insistently at a computer screen. "Set a course for the center of the Alconbury Nebula."

That was the name of the street we lived on when he was part of our lives. Alconbury Lane in Houston.

"I cannot recommend that course of action, sir. It is too dangerous and holds too many unpleasant memories."

Sol looks at me, his jaw agape and quivering, his eyes widening with rage. "ARE YOU DISOBEYING A DIRECT ORDER, COMMANDER? HOW DARE YOU! LIEUTENANT WORF, TAKE THIS MAN TO THE BRIG! AND BRING MY BELT! THIS IS GOING TO HURT ME MORE THAN IT DOES

YOU, BUT I'LL TEACH YOU A LESSON YOU'LL NEVER FORGET!"

I wake up yelling my head off. "No, please, sir! I'll be good! I promise!!!"

Glancing around in a panic, I'm relieved to find myself still in my own bed. When my breathing settles down, I piece together fragments of my dream, feeling grateful that Picard is the captain, and not my stepfather. Then I remember the message from the guy in Duluth. I need to talk to Cindy Lou. She'll tell me what to do. Picking up the phone, I notice my alarm clock and realize that it's still the middle of the night. Shit. I'll call her in the morning. Feeling vulnerable, I climb out of bed and grab my Joe DiMaggio slugger for protection, just in case. I open the shutters on the window and look out into the night. All I see in the darkness is the empty street in front of my house, illuminated by the lonely glow of a solitary streetlamp. In the canyon, a coyote howls. It sounds like a warning.

TWELVE

DOUBLE TROUBLE

AFTER MAKING A quick run for a bag of donut holes and a cup of coffee, I phone Cindy Lou and fill her in on last night's mysterious caller.

"Hmmm, that's interesting. He didn't give you his name?" she asks.

"No, just what I told you. And there was another letter from Lal in my trailer. There was blood on it."

"What did it say?"

"It was all about the razor blades and wanting to give me a shave. A close shave!"

"I don't like the sound of that," she says. "Lal is getting more specific. More threatening."

"Oh God, should I get a gun?"

"No," she says without pause.

"Do you have a gun?" I ask.

"Of course."

"Then why shouldn't I have one?"

"Do you know how to use a gun?"

"Well, I played a gunslinger at AstroWorld amusement park in Houston one summer."

"You just answered your own question."

I like this woman. She's smart. And she carries a gun. I've never known a woman that carries a gun . . . that I'm aware of.

"Hang on to that letter, and any others you get. I'll pick them up when I can. Also, it might be a good idea for you to hire a personal bodyguard. Could take some of the pressure off until we find this person."

"Really? Okay, but why can't you be my bodyguard?" I ask wistfully.

"I'm an FBI agent, Mr. Spiner. That's a completely different field. Besides, I'm on several active cases right now other than yours."

For some silly reason, I feel slightly rejected. "Of course, I just thought it might be fun to, you know, hang out a little bit," I say, fishing.

"We're not allowed to 'hang out' with anyone in the middle of an investigation."

There goes that fantasy.

"I think you'll like the bodyguard I have in mind," she offers. "You can decide how much protection you feel comfortable with. On the set. Guarding you at home. It's completely up to you."

"Who is this person? How do you know him?"

"Her. She's my sister."

"Your sister?" I ask.

"That's right. Private security consultant Candy Lou Jones. We came up in the FBI together, but she left to strike out on her own. You'll be in good hands. She's guarded several celebrities."

"Are all of them still with us?"

"Every single one."

"Okay, those are pretty solid numbers. But how will I know that she's your sister? What if the person who shows up is the stalker pretending to be your sister?"

"Oh, you'll know," she says coyly. "We're identical twins."

After arranging to meet her sister later at the studio, we agree to speak again in the next few days. Fully aware that I need nutrition for the sixteen-hour day ahead of me, I scarf down the remaining donut holes in the bag. I should know better than to eat them so ravenously. I once got one stuck in my throat and thought I was going to choke to death. Fortunately, I had enough composure to fling myself over the back of a dining room chair. It took three tries, but it finally exploded out of my craw like a doughy musket ball. It landed dead center on a print of a Vargas model hanging on my wall. It arrived with such force, I was never able to scrape the whole thing off, so now it looks like she has a huge belly button. An outie, to be specific.

Midafternoon at the studio, on a bench outside of Stage 9 running lines in my head, waiting to shoot a scene with Patrick. This is another of those historic spots film fanatics like me are humbled to be in the presence of. Part of Billy Wilder's immortal *Sunset Boulevard* was shot on this stage. The stairway, next to where I sit, is where William Holden jogged up to see his girl-friend in the writer's room. Sometimes I just have to pinch my-self. I light up a Marlboro Red and take the smoke deep into my lungs. Right, I started smoking again. I'm a little disappointed in myself since I just gave up cigarettes last week.

"What the hell is that?" asks LeVar, lighting up an Export 'A' of his own.

Michael Dorn and LeVar, having wrapped for the day, stop by on their way off the lot.

"Yeah, I've been looking for an excuse to start again," I say, exhaling a lungful and sucking it up my nose, French style. "I think the possibility of being murdered qualifies."

"See, something good comes from everything." LeVar chuck-les, ever the optimist.

"Guys," says Dorn, his basso voice matching the serious-ness of his intent, "you both need to quit! Don't you know what it does to your skin? And it makes you stink!"

These things are important to Dorn. At six-two and sans his Klingon makeup, he's easily the best-looking guy on the show. On many shows, for that matter. He's committed to preserving God's gift as long as possible.

"You want us to hang with you for a while?" offers LeVar.

"No, that's okay. My scene is up soon, and I'm waiting for someone. I'm meeting a personal bodyguard."

"A bodyguard!" they exclaim in unison.

"Yeah. Recommended by FBI agent Cindy Lou Jones. It's her twin sister, Candy Lou Jones."

They look at me as if I'm making it up, but I assure them

that she's real, even though, yes, it does sound like something out of *Playboy*'s Forum column. At that moment, a voice a few feet away grabs our attention.

"Mr. Spiner?" A woman in a tight black suit strides confidently toward me. She's a carbon copy of Cindy Lou Jones, with the exception of a sleek black bob instead of a sleek blond bob.

"Candy Lou Jones, I presume?"

"None other," she responds.

I'm completely astonished. She really is the mirror image of Cindy Lou, though slightly different in her style and posture. Genetics has also gifted her with those unmistakably sexy Veronica Lake kind of pipes. We shake hands and I introduce her to LeVar and Dorn, who seem as transfixed by the resemblance as I am.

"Wow, you really are the spittin' image of your sister," says LeVar to my one-woman protection detail.

If looks could kill, she fixes him with a deadly serious glare. "I wasn't made in her image," she counters. "She was made in mine."

We stare at her, not exactly sure what to make of that. Finally she lets us off the hook.

"Jeez, lighten up, guys. That was a joke. I was born first," she says, flashing a megawatt smile.

We laugh awkwardly. With raised eyebrows, LeVar and I give each other looks as if to say, *This is going to be interesting.*

"But you're far more beautiful than your sister," Dorn says, making the ever-familiar Dorn move.

"Smooth," she replies disdainfully, reducing Dorn from

six-two to a normal-sized schmuck. "Mr. Spiner, could I have a word with you in private?"

LeVar picks up the cue and cocks his head at Dorn, suggesting they vamoose.

"Nice to meet you, Miss Jones," LeVar says, tipping his finger to his brow. "Will we see you at the Roddenberrys' party, Spine?"

Gene Roddenberry, creator of *Star Trek*, and his wife, Majel, are giving one of their famous parties tonight. They love parties. The last one celebrated the release of the Hubble Space Telescope into Earth's orbit. Tonight's soiree commemorates Majel's first time breaking 120 strokes in eighteen holes at the Bel-Air Country Club. You gotta love them. Anything for a party.

"I don't know. I'd like to come, and Gene's parties are always so inter—"

"Bad idea," she says, cutting me off mid-sentence. "You should stay away from social gatherings for the time being, Mr. Spiner. It's not safe."

"Why don't you come with him?" Dorn suggests. "With your expertise, couldn't you prevent anyone dangerous from getting to him?"

"It's all about risk and probability, sir," she replies. "I probably could, but you never know."

She takes me by the arm and politely but firmly steers me away from LeVar and Dorn. Clearly, it's time to get down to business. We adjourn to my trailer, and after taking a seat on the couch, she pulls a sheet of paper from her inside coat pocket.

"This part is always a little uncomfortable," she says without the least sign of discomfort, "but the contract spells out everything very clearly. I charge forty-five dollars an hour, and I'll need a thousand-dollar retainer to begin."

"Wh . . . forty-five dollars an hour?" I gasp. "Damn, that could add up pretty quickly!"

"True. Just depends how much your life is worth to you," she says, offering me a pen.

Taking it from her and signing my name, I wonder to myself if bodyguards are tax deductible.

"You know, Miss Jones . . ."

"Call me Candy. I'm not as formal as my sister."

"Okay, uh, Candy. Listen, I'd really like to go to the party. I haven't had much fun lately."

She considers it for a moment. "Understand," she says, boring a hole into my soul with her baby blues. "My job—and my sister's job—is to preserve your life. And we take our jobs very seriously."

"I appreciate that. But I can't just hide out in my house all the time. Couldn't we go for just a little while?"

"How long are you thinking?" she asks, not particularly crazy about the idea.

"Oh, I don't know. Maybe around ninety dollars' worth."

"Okay, it's your call." She sighs. "You're the boss. But if I say get the fuck down, GET THE FUCK DOWN."

I nod enthusiastically. I happen to be very good at taking direction.

THIRTEEN   THE PARTY

HAVING INSISTED ON driving me, Candy Lou Jones arrives at my house in a 1977 vintage black Buick Regal. When I open the front door, she stands there wearing a form-fitted black evening dress, hair slicked back, looking like she just stepped out of a *Vanity Fair* photo shoot with Annie Leibovitz. Even though I donned my best suit for the occasion, I give the unfortunate impression of something out of a JCPenney catalogue.

"Wow, you're a knockout, Miss Jones," I say with utter sincerity, hoping she returns the compliment.

She looks me up and down and responds with her version of kindness. "If you're a good boy, I'll take you shopping someday. Free of charge. C'mon, let's roll."

Opening the door of the back passenger side, she directs me to get in. She slides behind the wheel, flicks the locks shut, and we're off. From the back seat I find myself staring at her perfect profile, her gleaming black hair, her muscular shoulders.

Gotta say, there's something captivating about these Jones women.

"So how'd you get into bodyguarding, Candy?"

"Always in my blood. Cindy and I used to protect each other at school. It was a rough neighborhood. We were constantly being picked on by bullies, so we took karate classes in the afternoon and things changed dramatically. It was very satisfying."

"I'll bet," I said, conjuring up an image of the two of them roughing up a bunch of rowdies with a series of groin kicks. "Boy, I know about bullies. A kid in Hebrew school used to yank my yarmulke off every day and sail it across the room like a Frisbee. But I put a stop to that."

"What'd you do?" she asked.

"I told him if he'd cut it out, I'd write his bar mitzvah speech for him. Worked like a charm."

She turned her head and shot me a look of pity that I'll never forget.

"Anyway, my sister and I went to the same college and majored in criminal justice," she continued. "After graduation, we both applied to the FBI, went to training school, and became agents. But I wasn't satisfied with doing investigations. I wanted to be in personal security at the Secret Service. It wasn't easy in those days. Typical boys' club. I had dreams of being on Reagan's detail, but no way would they let that happen. Then in '81, after he was shot by Hinckley, I was so pissed off, knowing I could've prevented him from taking that bullet, that I quit and became a private security consultant and bodyguard for people like you."

"Lucky me!" I say, making eye contact in the rearview mirror.

"No shit," she replies confidently.

We pull up to Gene Roddenberry's home, a gorgeous mansion in the hills of Bel Air. Candy Lou pulls the car up to the closed gate and presses a button on a speaker box. A voice comes over the speaker.

"Roddenberry residence."

"Brent Spiner plus one," says Candy Lou.

"Yes, drive in, please."

The gate opens and we proceed up the long drive onto the property. Candy Lou, ever the professional, waits until it closes behind us. Arriving at the front entrance to the house, she turns the car over to the valet.

"Keep her close and there's a Hamilton in it for you. We won't be staying long."

The front door opens, revealing a smiling Gene Roddenberry, glass of white wine in hand. Gene is a large man with large appetites of many varieties. Use your imagination. He certainly does. In fairness, he's always been incredibly sweet to me. Grandfatherly, in a way. I like him.

"Come in, come in! So glad you could make it! And who is this lovely young woman?" he asks.

"Oh, forgive me. Gene Roddenberry, this is Candy Lou Jones."

"Candy! What a charming name! You know the saying 'Candy is dandy, but liquor is quicker!'" he says, downing the remainder of his drink.

Nothing like a little Ogden Nash to break the ice.

"Gene, Candy is my bodyguard. I don't know if you're aware of what's been—"

"Oh yes, indeed, I've been fully apprised of the situation. Smart of you to travel with a 'hired gun.'"

He knows the territory. Gene was an officer in the LAPD back in the day, hopefully nothing like the dreaded Ortiz.

"I used to have an unusual fan of my own," he continues. "Try as I might, I couldn't get her to leave me alone."

"What did you do?" I ask, leaning in for wisdom from the "Great Bird of the Galaxy."

"I married her! Best decision of my life! Let's go see if we can find her. I know she'd like to say hello."

He escorts us through open French doors to the backyard, which has been decked out in full party mode. Huge bouquets of flowers adorn a dozen round dining tables draped with white tablecloths. The grounds are illuminated by several fire pits and hundreds of candles of different sizes. Tuxedoed servers stroll about offering various delicacies on trays. The Roddenberrys' German shepherd Khan, named after the Ricardo Montalbán character in the movie *The Wrath of Khan*, bounds from person to person begging for a canapé. A group of guests are huddled around a fully stocked bar at the side of the property. And that's where we find Gene's wife, Majel, the First Lady of Star Trek, holding court and making history of a double cosmopolitan.

"Look at her. Isn't she something?" Gene whispers to us as we approach.

"I believe that's a rhetorical question, Gene."

He appreciates my political response with a hearty chuckle. She is clearly the love of his life and he supports her every whim. Not only has he set her up with a company that sells a multitude of Star Trek memorabilia, she also has a couple of recurring roles on our show: the voice of the ship's computer and most notably, Lwaxana Troi, mother of Counselor Deanna Troi (Marina Sirtis).

"Darling!" he says, interrupting her conversation and slipping his long arm around her waist. "Look who's here. Our favorite android and his lovely . . . date."

I steal a look to Candy to see how that description sits with her. She cocks her head as if to say, *whatever.* Majel greets us both with a kiss to each cheek and casually grabs my ass as she is wont to do. I'm certain Gene clocks that move, but I think it amuses rather than upsets him. Majel introduces us to some of the people at the bar, one of whom turns out to be Buzz Aldrin of moonshot fame. Pretty impressive. Scanning the crowd in hopes of seeing a familiar face, I happily discover that the rest of my cast of comrades have already arrived. Patrick, hand in hand with a woman I've never met, approaches and greets me with a hug and a kiss on the cheek. That's the way men in show business greet each other. I've never been completely comfortable with it, but that's my problem.

"Brent, I'm so glad you came!" he bellows in that unmistakable voice. "And look at you, Agent Jones. Black hair is very becoming on you."

"Oh no, Patrick, this isn't Agent Cindy Lou Jones," I explain. "This is my bodyguard, Candy Lou Jones. They're sisters."

"Excellent disguise," he says, and winks conspiratorially. "And I'd like you to meet my new friend, Miss Katherine Segal. Katherine is a *wonderful* architect. She's already been featured in *Los Angeles Magazine* as someone to keep your eye on. And that's exactly what I plan to do."

They share a kiss, and something tells me he'll be seeing a lot more of her before the evening is over. When they un-clinch, she gazes up at the house and sighs.

"Isn't this place something?" she says. "The great architect Paul Williams designed it for Cary Grant and Barbara Hutton when they were married in the early forties. I've seen pictures of it when it was first built. It was gorgeous."

"Still is," I add, not knowing shit about architecture.

"Have you been inside?" she asks. "They completely re-modeled. Fucked it up! Goddamn Philistines! It's like paint-ing a tube top on the Mona Lisa. C'mon, babe," she says to Patrick. "Let's get a drink."

Patrick hangs back a moment as she heads for the bar. "Be right there, darling. Order me a Bushmills on the rocks, would you?"

Turning to us, he shrugs his shoulders and adds, "She can be very difficult. But what the hell, she's absolutely adorable. Excuse me, won't you?"

Dinner is served, so Candy and I find a couple of empty seats at one of the tables. Our dining partners for the evening include Michael Dorn, Marina and her husband, a couple of dinosaurs from the Bel-Air Country Club, and to my everlasting pleasure, Anne Jeffreys and Robert Sterling. This glamorous married couple from the golden days of Hollywood was central to my youthful fascination with movies and television.

"Oh my God," I say to Candy, "did you ever see the television series *Topper*?"

"Sure, who didn't?"

"Well, that's George 'that most sporty spirit' Kerby and his wife, Marion, the 'ghostess with the mostest'!"

"Oh yeah," she says, remembering. "Gee, they're still so beautiful!"

As a beet and avocado salad is placed in front of each of us, Majel taps a spoon against the side of her glass to capture the party's collective attention.

"I have a wonderful surprise for everyone," she announces. "Our dear friends, Anne Jeffreys and Robert Sterling, have been rehearsing a new nightclub act and have graciously agreed to perform a number for us. So c'mon, let's hear it for them!"

After a healthy round of applause, Sterling takes his wife by the hand and they stand at their seats. Following a few lines of charming patter, they launch into a pitch-perfect a cappella rendition of Frank and Nancy Sinatra's "Somethin' Stupid." Actually makes a lot more sense than Frank and Nancy's version. I always wondered why a guy would sing romantic stuff like that to his own daughter. Anyway, it's moments like this that cement my love of Hollywood. And for the first time in a long time, I'm overflowing with happiness. My friends are here. I'm rubbing shoulders with old-time stars. And, yes, Candy is by my side making me feel safe.

Khan, the wonder dog, nudges my leg and looks at me with

pleading eyes. Taking pity on the hungry hound, I toss a beet into the air, which he snaps up like a starving prisoner. Grateful, and hoping for more of my generosity, he plops down next to me. As I pinch another beet from my plate, a slightly familiar voice calls out from behind me.

"Brent! Hey!"

Turning to respond, I'm shocked, but thankfully not frightened, to see Todd. Guest star Todd.

"Todd!" I say, trying to disguise my surprise. "How nice to see you. Are you here with Gates?"

"No, I'm here with my new girlfriend. I give golf lessons to Mrs. Roddenberry, and she was kind enough to invite us."

"Oh, that's great! Seems those lessons are really paying off," I offer, hoping he doesn't see through my bullshit.

"I want you to meet my girlfriend. Honey!" he calls out. "Come here a minute."

A towering raven-haired beauty appears out of nowhere and presses herself against Todd. Holy shit, it's Mandy. Yes, *that* Mandy.

"Sweetheart," Todd coos, "this is Brent Spiner, one of my favorite actors and a terrific guy."

"Oh yes, we've met," she says, as if she barely knows me.

Doing my damnedest not to puke, I smile and greet her as cordially as I can. Todd, looking at her rapturously and having no idea he'll be toast in a couple of weeks, continues.

"Mandy and I met at one of my presentations at the actors' home. She came along with one of my regular readers and went home with me. It was just one of those things, as the song says. She's such a good person. So kind," he says, kissing her on the temple.

"So, Brent, are you still dealing with your little problem? I mean, are we safe with you here?" Mandy asks, her eyes crossing slightly.

"Don't worry, Mandy, you're safe. In fact, I'd like you to meet my bodyguard. Mandy, this is Candy."

They eye each other suspiciously and shake hands.

"Pleased to meet you," says Mandy

"Charmed," Candy replies.

At that moment, the servers begin removing the salads, and plates of the traditional breast of chicken with julienned vegetables take their place.

"Oooh, that looks yummy. C'mon, sweetheart, I'm starving," says Mandy, urging Todd to their table.

As they start off, I stop Todd. "Todd, one last thing. Not that it matters, but I think you should know. She says prima pasta vera."

"What?" he asks, utterly confused.

"Oh, fuck it, never mind. Have a nice evening."

As Todd joins Mandy, I grab my knife and raise it with the intention of sharing my foul mood with a piece of chicken.

Placing a supportive hand on my arm, Candy cautions me. "Take it easy, pal. You don't want to make a scene."

"You're right," I say, turning to her. "I was feeling so good, and then Mandy has to show up."

"Have some vegetables. They're good for your blood pressure."

Reaching for my fork, I notice that the breast of chicken is no longer on my plate. I look to my right and see Khan happily chowing down on my dinner. For some reason, I find this funny—that is, until the dog's legs begin to wobble. Suddenly he spasms and drops onto his side like a seventy-pound bag of Purina Puppy Chow.

"Oh my God," I say, panic-stricken. "Candy, the dog ate my chicken and dropped dead! Someone poisoned the chicken! That was meant for me!"

In a blur, Candy is on her feet, gun in hand. Where it came from, I have no idea.

"Nobody moves!" she shouts, loud enough for the entire party to hear. Addressing one of the servers, she orders, "I want everyone from the kitchen out here. NOW!"

As the terrified server runs to the kitchen to fetch the rest of the help, Majel stands and sees her beloved pet comatose on the patio. "Khhhhaaaaaannnnn!" she shrieks, sounding eerily like William Shatner in the aforementioned film.

Throwing off his jacket and loosening his tie, Michael Dorn charges toward the helpless animal.

"I said don't move!" Candy warns, pointing the pistol in his direction.

"Stand down, lady. I used to be in veterinary school before I became an actor," Dorn reveals.

That in fact may be the biggest revelation of the evening. Candy lowers her weapon and steps back, giving Dorn room to operate. He rolls the dog over onto its back and begins chest compressions. Nothing. He pries open the mutt's muzzle and considers, for a brief moment, giving mouth-to-mouth. Thinking better of it, he wraps his arms around the dog's chest and places a fist just below its rib cage. Wrapping his other hand tightly over his fist, Dorn administers three robust pumps to Khan's midsection. On the third attempt, Khan emits a guttural hacking sound, and a breast of chicken, completely intact, propels onto my lap. For a moment, nobody moves or speaks. I look to Candy, feeling simultaneously embarrassed, relieved, and just the slightest bit grossed out at having a chicken breast perched on my crotch. And admittedly, I empathize with the poor creature, having experienced a similar humiliation with a donut hole.

"It wasn't poison," I squeak out weakly.

Majel runs to her dog and caresses it lovingly as the dog, no doubt happy to be alive, licks her face, leaving a slight residue of chicken fat on her cheeks. Candy holsters her weapon in some hidden place and congratulates Dorn on a job well done.

"Folks," she explains as she turns to the horrified partygoers, "sorry for the drama. Luckily this was a false alarm. I'm paid to protect this man, and that's what I intend to do. Now go ahead and enjoy your dinner."

Taking a napkin from the table, she gingerly plucks the chicken breast from my groin and tosses it on the table. Looking me in the eyes, she says with absolute certainty, "It's time to say good night."

FOURTEEN   IT WAS HIS BIRTHDAY

AS THE SUN rises in the west, I awake alone in my own bed. Having gotten us safely home last night, Candy Lou Jones is getting forty winks in my guest room. She told me that she sleeps with her gun under her pillow and has trained herself to wake up at the slightest sound, so my safety is assured, even while she's seemingly fast asleep. I don't hear any snoring, so that's probably a good sign.

When she wakes up, I make us coffee and then she drives us to Paramount Studios, where I find a new letter waiting for me in my trailer. It's kind of reassuring to get a letter with someone there by my side, rather than totally alone.

Dear Brent,

Did you call me last night? I believe that was you. I would know your voice anywhere. Oh my! I am still in a state of shock! No one has ever talked to me like that. Not even Andrew. The things you said were SO NAUGHTY. I suppose you Hollywood people talk like that all the time. But as a Christian woman, I have never heard anything like that. Certainly not in church! Ha-ha. I go to church as often as I can. I have conversations with the pastor there. Pastor Hope is very kind, and our talks always make me feel better. But not what I felt last night. My heart was literally beating out of my chest. It was so exciting. I loved it!!! I hope Jesus will forgive me for what I was thinking about us.

Why didn't you answer when I asked if it was you? I mean, I understand, I think. You have to be careful. You're a very famous person and you have to protect yourself. Also, I am a married woman and you wouldn't want any trouble from my husband. Don't worry. I would never tell him. I would never do anything to harm you.

I would never harm anyone. As I said in my other letter, we used to live in North Carolina, but we had to leave the country. Canada is so cold! I prefer a warm climate. Penny, that's my child, and I stay inside the apartment most of the time. I don't speak to the neighbors. They can be very nosy. I don't want any more problems like before, so I try to use the laundry room after midnight when no one else is there.

Have I told you too much about me? I don't know why, but I trust you and want to talk to you. Star Trek is a kinder and more understanding world. Especially Data.

Andrew will be gone for the next two weeks. Please feel free to call me again. We can talk about anything you want. It doesn't have to be like last night. But I wouldn't

be mad if you talked to me that way again. I hope you
call me. And very soon.

I just wish my husband was dead.

Affectionately,
Loretta Gibson

"How many letters have you received from this person?"
Candy asks.

"This is the third," I say.

"She could be dangerous."

"I don't know. It's so confusing. Not only is she imagin-
ing that I'm calling her late at night and having graphic sexual conversations, now she wants her husband dead? Jesus
Christ, how did I get involved in all this crap?

"Or is she playing you?" Candy thinks aloud. "Is Loretta
your stalker?"

Silently lost in our own thoughts, we both consider the pos-
sibilities. And then the phone rings.

"Hello?"

"Hi, Brent, it's your mother."

Of course it is.

My mother is quite a remarkable woman. Part little girl,
part lioness. Whichever suits the situation. Her life has been
filled with challenges, particularly in the area of love. But
with each catastrophe, she rises like a phoenix from the ashes.
She's gone from being a widow with two babies at the age of
twenty-three to vice-president of a large corporation. Granted,
it's my grandfather's company, but he believed in starting at

the bottom and working your way up. And through grit and determination, she did precisely that. At one time or another, most of my family has been a part of "the business." It never interested me. I was much more attracted to being a starving actor and facing a daily wall of rejection. I'm funny that way. But my mother didn't have the luxury of exploration. She had kids to support. She is well liked for her sweet personality and very respected within her professional community. And to me—well, to me, she's my Jewish mother. Always available with endless encouragement, an unwanted opinion, and a damn fine bowl of matzo ball soup.

"Hi, Mom."

Candy, sensitive to my need for privacy, indicates she'll be outside.

"Are you all right?" my mother asks in her serious voice.

She always sounds different when she's calling from work. She uses her business voice. More vice-presidential and less motherly.

"I'm fine."

"Are you?" she asks, obviously sensing that I'm not.

"I'm fine! C'mon," I say, trying to sound chipper.

Is there ever a profit in telling your mother that someone is obsessed with killing you?

"Then, I'm guessing you haven't heard? I . . . I hate having to tell you this."

Oh no. I was wrong. It's not her business voice. It's her "something terrible has happened" voice.

"What? What is it, Mom?" I ask, not actually wanting an answer.

"Trey died."

"What? Oh my God, no! How?"

"He had a brain aneurysm. It was his birthday. He was getting dressed to go out and celebrate and he suddenly got a blinding headache. His wife called an ambulance, but by the time they got to the hospital, he was gone."

Trey. Trey Wilson. Donald Yearnsley Wilson III. One of my closest friends. We met in high school drama class. He was a year ahead of me, but we bonded instantly. Later he was my roommate in college. I was best man in his wedding. We wrote together, did plays together, and dreamed together. And his dreams had just started to come true. He'd just begun to explode as a major talent with leading roles in the films *Raising Arizona* and *Bull Durham*. And now, just like that, he's gone. How can this be real? Hearing this news is like getting punched in the stomach. I can't breathe. I sit down, nauseous and dizzy. The room is spinning and my mother is still on the line. I try to keep it together.

"When . . . when is the funeral?"

"It's on Sunday."

"I'll fly home tomorrow. Can you pick me up at the airport?"

"Of course. Let me know when your plane is arriving."

"Mom, I can't talk anymore."

"I understand. I'm so sorry. Goodbye, dear. I love you."

When she hangs up, I crumble and weep deeply for my friend, thinking about the impact he had on my life, how I'm never going to see him again, how much I loved him. I sob uncontrollably for the first time in years. A self-imposed wall I'd built long ago finally collapses. And oddly I am overwhelmed with guilt, because at this horrible time, having reclaimed that part of myself, I feel whole.

✳

Trey's funeral is a somber affair. It is packed with friends, our teachers, our parents—all devastated. Those of us who were closest to him serve as pallbearers. Afterward, Judy, his wife, invites us to her mother's house to be together, to tell stories, to remember everything about him. Trey is the first friend I've lost, and it seems impossible. I drive home in silence with my mother, to her apartment, and climb into my old bed. Everything is familiar, but forever changed.

I dream about Trey in drama class.

We're performing a scene together playing brothers in the Civil War. Both of us have been stabbed by bayonets, and we hold each other close as we die. His acting is much better than mine. After he dies, he springs back to life at the applause of the class and smiles with his whole being. He loves acting, and he loves the work of acting. He devours life. Trey loves living more than I do. And yet I'm alive and he's dead. I watch him and feel grateful to know him.

Then, as happens in dreams, everything transforms, and I'm watching something else entirely.

My brother and I are at the dining room table doing our homework. My mother comes home from work and starts to make dinner.

It looks like it's going to be sukiyaki, one of her specialties. My stepfather, Sol, sashays into the room and puts a Rosemary Clooney record on the phonograph. He pulls my mother close to him and they dance slowly, romantically. They are both excellent dancers. They seem happy in this moment, and that pleases me. It's as if the music is alive, lifting us into its arms, out of our normally troubled reality. The one good thing I got from Sol was my love of great music. At least he gave me that. Rosie sings:

> *Your arms opened wide*
> *And closed me inside.*
> *You took my lips*
> *You took my love*
> *So tenderly.*

FIFTEEN

STRIKING DISTANCE

ARRIVING BACK IN L.A. in the early evening, I put in a call to Candy Lou and ask if she's available to stay with me overnight. I'm still a little shaky and her presence would help to take the edge off. Thankfully she agrees and shows up at my door in no time. As she makes up the couch in the guest room, I can feel the last few days of tension begin to melt away. She makes me feel less afraid, less vulnerable. I'll sleep peacefully tonight for a change. I wonder if she has a weekly rate for sleepovers?

When I wake in the morning, I hear Candy making breakfast in the kitchen and singing softly. Such a sweet sound. I could definitely get used to this. The cooking bodyguard? Pretty unbeatable combination. She brings a plate of eggs and a cup of coffee into my room and sets them on the bedside table.

"We're a full-service operation," she says, smiling.

She sits on the side of the bed and fixes me with a look. The top of her robe falls open slightly, and it's all I can do not to take a cursory peek. But her eyes are so focused on mine that I'm afraid she'd catch me. And then where would we be?

"I've been thinking about how we're going to win against this stalker," she says. "Maybe we're going about this the wrong way. Maybe it's not such a good idea to keep you under wraps."

"I don't know, I'm not hating being here."

"If she finds out where you live, she's sure to come here. But that could take weeks. Or months. Even years. Is that what you want? To spend your life living in fear? Always wondering when you'll hear the clicking sound of a gun preparing to fire?"

"Wait, wait. You said *she*. What makes you think this is a woman?"

A sly smile lights up her face. "I know my business," she replies with an appealing arrogance, "and I'm rarely wrong."

"What exactly are you proposing?" I ask.

"We need to get you out there, in public. Draw her to us," she says, her brain cells firing on all cylinders.

"Well, I've agreed to be at a Star Trek convention in San Diego this weekend. But I was going to cancel."

"No," she interrupts, "this is great! If she knows you're coming, there's every chance she'll be there. Let's be proactive and put a stop to this nightmare. Are you with me?"

"I want to be, but honestly, the thought of being within striking distance scares the shit out of me."

She scootches up the bed a bit and leans her head in close to mine. "Don't worry, baby," she murmurs softly, "I won't let anything happen to you."

Our faces move closer, our lips mere inches apart. Every fiber of my being wants to take her in my arms and kiss her. And maybe, just maybe, a few of her fibers are thinking the same thing. We seem frozen in a tableau of desire. At last she breaks from the excruciating stillness of the moment and grabs the plate of eggs next to us.

"Let's go to San Diego," she says, gobbling down a couple of mouthfuls. And then, that smile.

Before heading down, we stop at the studio to pick up my pictures for the convention. There are boxes of photos in my trailer of Data in various poses. Action Data. Data looking quizzically into the universe, Data as Sherlock Holmes. At these conventions, I sit at a table while the fans line up in front of me, waiting for their turn to purchase my autograph at prices well beyond their worth. Most of us dismiss this thievery with the justification that no one is actually forced to buy anything. It's their choice. But to my mind, they are not really interested in the signed pictures at all. It's the connection. So I do my best to give them a moment to remember. Something they can take with them that makes their time and money seem worth it. When we get into my trailer, I find that Mickey has dropped off today's mail, a disappointingly meager amount. What the hell? I thought I was more popular than that? I grab the small stack and begin counting my take, hoping Candy doesn't notice my disgusting vanity. And there it is. Another one. The same precise handwriting. No return address.

"Candy—"

"Open it," she says, registering the envelope, as well as the pained expression on my face.

I tear it open and withdraw the letter, already well aware of the gist of its contents.

Dear Daddy,

How's my yiddishe papa feeling today? I just wanted you to know that I can't wait to see you at the convention. I hope you're still planning on being there. Marina's going too, isn't she? What fun. But don't worry. If you've changed your mind, I'd be happy to kill Marina instead.
See you in San Diego.

Your loving daughter,
Lal

"This is perfect," Candy says, clapping her hands together with a touch too much glee.

"Enlighten me. How is this perfect? She actually says she wants to kill me!"

"We know she's going to be there. This is our chance to get her."

"Yeah, but I don't know, I'm not sure I can do this. I mean, what if we don't see her and she sneaks up on me and she has a gun or a knife? And you're looking the other way, and . . . and . . . what if you're wrong and it's not a woman? What if she's a man, a big man—"

Whack! She slaps me hard across the face.

"Get ahold of yourself!" she demands.

In the movies, in scenes like this, the person who takes the blow usually says, "Thanks, I needed that." In point of fact, I would've preferred she just shush me. Nonetheless, I regain my composure.

"Okay. Just don't hit me again," I say, rubbing the sting from my cheek.

"I need you there. And I need you to be brave." she says, placing a conciliatory arm around my shoulder. "Now, why don't you give Marina a call and give her a heads-up."

She's right. I need to warn Marina. Marina Sirtis, a British American actress of Greek extraction, plays the ship's counselor on the show, Deanna Troi. Troi is particularly adroit at assisting the ship's population with their psychological issues, in part because she is an empath; she is able to sense thoughts and feelings. Ironically, Marina is gifted with some of these qualities in her real life. Yet as perceptive as she is, I'm sure she never saw this one coming. Hoping she hasn't already left, I pick up the phone and dial her number.

"Hallo," comes a distinctly Cockney voice through the receiver.

"Marina, it's Brent."

"Hi, Brento! Are you already in San Diego?"

"No, I had to pick up my pictures at Paramount. Listen, Marina, I have to tell you something a little upsetting. You know this stalker thing I've been going through? Lal? Well, I just got another letter from her, and this one says if I'm not at the convention, that she'd be happy to kill you."

"Oh, I see. Well then, why are you dillydallying? Get your ass down there!"

She brushes this news off with a laugh. I wish I could join her.

"This is serious, Marina. I'd hate myself if anything happened to you."

"Oh, don't get your knickers in a knot. If he comes after me or you, I'll kick him in the balls!"

"Oh yeah? What if Lal is a woman?"

"Same. She'd have to have balls to fuck with me! I'll see you there, darling."

She hangs up. I marvel at her courage. I guess years of getting into fistfights at the soccer matches of Tottenham Hotspur, her beloved team, has given her a sense of invincibility. And I'm actually quite touched at how my friends have tried to take care of me under such extreme circumstances. You can be sure I'll remember that if anyone ever wants to kill them.

Candy and I drive to San Diego and pull into the VIP parking area of the Ulysses S. Grant Hotel, an old landmark in the heart of downtown. We're met and escorted to a holding room by a trio of the promoter's staff, all costumed as various Star Trek aliens. I notice Candy taking them in with a quizzical expression on her face. Maybe she thinks one of them is Lal. Or maybe she just thinks they look peculiar. We're told to enjoy a cornucopia of unappetizing snacks until a healthy line builds up and we can do some business. As I get a large bottle of water from the refrigerator, Candy excuses herself and heads to a nearby restroom. Makes me think. What if I need to use the men's room and Lal is lurking there, waiting to pounce on me from one of the stalls? Maybe it's best I not challenge my bladder. I put the water back. When Candy returns, I can hardly believe my eyes. She has changed into a different outfit. A red Starfleet officer's miniskirt uniform. Security, naturally.

"I thought it would be a good idea to blend in," she says.

"That'll be the day," I reply, doing my best not to reach out and straighten the slightly crooked communicator badge above her left breast.

Before long, I'm seated at my table signing autographs in front of an oversize poster of Data, who hovers behind me with folded arms, a fake protector TV god who will literally do nothing if danger rears his or her ugly head. Fortunately, I have my trusty bottle of Purell to ward off unwanted germs, and Candy sitting next to me to ward off unwanted killers. She is also serving as my "handler" today, taking the money for my autograph and making change when needed. It's always best that I not handle the filthy lucre myself. Not a good look. The giant ballroom is a virtual circus of Star Trek. Vendor booths peddle Star Trek action figures, photographs, comic books, trading cards, uniforms—a huge assortment of useless but irresistible merchandise. A food court is crowded with people enjoying a variety of fast-food delicacies sure to terminate their lives long before nature intended. Hundreds of devoted fans of all shapes and sizes fill the room, many in costume and makeup, some dressed as totally obscure characters from episodes I don't even remember. This is their

Xanadu, a safe space free of judgment, ablaze with their own personal creativity. And the curious are here as well. Moms and Pops with their kids, come to find out what the heck this screwy petri dish of humanity is all about. It is, if nothing else, a sight to behold.

Candy does her double duty effortlessly, exchanging pleasantries with the fans while covertly scanning for would-be assassins. So far all of these folks are friendly, kind, smart, and funny, exactly the people who, if I'm not mistaken, will one day inherit the earth. First in line for an up-close-and-personal moment, as they are at almost every convention I attend, are the Taylor twins, Jack and Jake. They are somewhere in their thirties, and exceptionally tall, somewhere north of the six-foot area. They are from New Zealand and both work in a secondary school, one teaching science and the other teaching math. How they get the money to travel the world several times a year, I do not know. Each time we meet, they share with me the catastrophe that's just befallen their darling mother. And each revelation involves the loss of another of her extremities, reminiscent of Lemuel Pitkin, the pathetic main character of Nathanael West's novel *A Cool Million*.

"Oh, Brent," Jack says, shaking his head, "it's awful. Mum has just had to have her left leg removed above the knee. It's such a blow to her after having just had the right one taken off last year."

"Oh, I'm so sorry. I can't imagine," I respond.

"And after losing both arms just three years ago," adds Jake, "she's really just a torso now. Just a large stump in a chair. So sad. At least she can't get at the whiskey anymore. But we try to get over there and feed her as often as time allows."

"You're . . . you're good sons," I say uncomfortably.

I have to assume someone feeds her while they're away at conventions.

"She's such a fighter. She still has that angelic smile, despite the fact that all of her teeth are gone."

Tempted as I am to ask how all of these calamities have befallen her, my line is growing, and I fear a tale of epic proportions.

"Guys, I'm so sorry to hear this. Please, give your mum this picture from me, will you?"

I reach for one of the Data photos and sign it *All my love, Brent.* I realize that's an insincere thing to write. I mean, how can you give all of your love to someone you don't even know? But that's the best I can think of under the circumstances. This is the thing about being a "celebrity." There's no way you can please everyone or be sincere with everyone or respond to everyone's phone calls, so no matter what, eventually you're going to fall short and disappoint. And that makes my own neurosis even more complex. As much as I want to be loved by everyone, I don't want the responsibility of loving everyone in return.

"That is so lovely of you, Brent. She'll adore it. We'll put it in a frame for her."

And as they amble away, they wave and say in unison, "We love you, Brent."

Why on earth these brothers feel it's necessary to circumvent the globe to share their woes with me, I'm not sure. In some strange way, I guess they regard me as family. Everyone needs to feel that someone cares, and when you show up in their living rooms on a weekly basis, it creates a kind of bonding. That connection, again. At least I think that's what it is, and I suppose that's okay. But the line between affection and obsession can be wafer-thin. Just ask Lal.

I look over at Candy, who has been observing this unusual exchange with a bemused look.

"Twins," I say to her, "they're all so strange."

I can see she doesn't want to, but she smiles and looks away.

A young boy of around twelve years old, dressed as Data, approaches, and after choosing from one of the stacks of photos laid out on the table, he shyly speaks up. "Could I have your autograph, please?"

"Oh my gosh, are you Data?" I say, gently pulling his leg.

"No, *you're* Data." He giggles.

"Are you sure? You look an awful lot like Data to me."

He giggles again and looks at his feet. "No, I'm Stevie. I'm just dressed like Data."

Smiling, I sign his photo *To Stevie, my favorite boy in the universe,* and hand it back.

He admires it for a moment, then looks up and remembers something. "Oh, also, Lal asked me to give this to you." He holds out an envelope.

"What did you say?" I inquire, hoping I heard him wrong.

"Lal asked me to give this to you," he repeats, waiting for me to relieve him of the forbidden fruit.

Candy overhears and nods for me to take it. She stands behind me and together we silently read its contents.

Daddy.

I'm here and so are you but I'm the only one leaving here alive. By the way, I'm really sorry about Uncle Trey. I saw him last night and he said to tell you to stop messing with his wife. Wink wink.

Lal

My face grows instantly hot with a combination of fear and intense anger. Hate, even. How dare this person! It's one thing to terrorize me, and quite another to invade and make light of my personal grief. I always wanted to stop her. Now I want revenge.

"Where is the person who gave you this?" Candy asks the boy. "Can you point them out?"

"I dunno." The boy looks around. "I think they left."

"Do you remember what the person looked like?" I chime in.

"You know, like in that episode, uh, 'The Offspring'?"

"Like the young woman that I built? That Data built? Lal?" I asked him softly, trying not to scare him.

"No, like before you made her into a girl. She was, like, this other thing," he recalls.

"You mean like the shiny, pinkish gold person?" I ask, sounding ridiculous even to myself.

Candy comes around the table and takes the boy gently by the shoulders. "When this person spoke, Stevie, did they sound like a man or a woman?"

"Neither. It didn't talk. It just held up a card that said, *Please give this to Data.*"

I scan the crowd, looking for someone that looks like Lal before she became a human woman.

"Wait, what exactly are we looking for?" Candy asks. "A shiny, pinkish . . . what?"

"A shiny, pinkish gold, genderless, featureless android," I reply. "You know, like in 'The Offspring.'"

"Sorry, sugar, I don't watch the show." she says without the least bit of regret. "But I get the idea. Let's go."

She grabs my hand and we race around the ballroom, looking in every direction as we seek our prey. We pass Klingons, Romulans, even a wide variety of Spocks, but no Lal. Suddenly I see it. A pinkish gold genderless, featureless android. It stands casually sipping from a straw in a soft drink cup, through a hole in its face where its lips are supposed to be.

"Over there! That's Lal!" I yell to Candy Lou.

As we charge toward the pre-female Lal, a crowd gathers around us, taking pictures, reaching out for handshakes, and impeding our forward progress. Candy politely moves them aside as I repeat, "Bathroom break!" like a fool and push ahead. Coming up behind the pinkish gold, genderless, featureless android, Candy springs into action. She grabs the creature by the scruff of the neck and forces its faceless head against a nearby wall. Then she instinctively snatches her weapon from the holster on her hip, momentarily forgetting that it's a phaser and not a pistol. I could tell her, but why spoil the fun?

"Don't move or I'll blow a hole in you big enough to fly a spaceship through!" she commands, getting into the spirit of the convention.

Craning its head to get a better look at us, I see a flicker of recognition in its eyes. A familiar and decidedly male voice emerges tentatively from the characterless face. "Brent? What are you doing? It's me, Leonard!"

The voice most certainly belongs to the actor Leonard Crofoot, who originally portrayed the pre-female Lal on the show. Realizing our mistake, Candy quickly releases him from captivity, spinning her phaser like a six-gun back into its holster.

"Leonard, I'm so sorry. We thought . . . it's too complicated to explain. Just please, forgive me," I beg.

"No worries," he replies, ever the good sport. "I'm doing a panel, 'Minor Characters Speak.' It starts in five minutes. I should probably go sign in."

"Of course. And again, apologies. By the way, have I mentioned how great you look? You haven't changed a day."

"Thanks," he responds, pleased with the compliment. "I'm kind of disappointed, though. I thought I'd be the only one here in this outfit, but I saw another."

"Where? How long ago?" Candy interrupts.

"About fifteen minutes ago, that way."

He gestures back toward the signing area. I quickly wish Leonard the best for his panel, and Candy Lou and I push our way back through the throngs, desperately combing the area for Lal. After an hour of searching, we give up and go back to my autograph table. Everyone has gone, having given up on getting an autograph from me. They probably went to see Leonard's panel. We find Marina still signing for a few fans and fill her in on what's been happening. I'm relieved for her that Lal appears to have left the building. Though, personally, I'm slightly disappointed.

"It makes me crazy that Lal mentioned Trey's name in that letter," I share with Candy.

"I understand," she replies. "That was cruel. There was something else in that letter. Did you notice? Who else said *wink wink* in a letter?"

"Loretta. Do you think she's Lal?"

"We'll find out soon enough."

As we walk through the hall to exit the building, we pass a man dressed as the character played on the original *Star Trek* by the great impressionist Frank Gorshin. His face is painted half white and half black. It was Roddenberry's comment on racism. I'm struck by this bizarre bit of solipsism: someone impersonating an impressionist. What a world.

We drive home from San Diego the long way, up the Pacific Coast Highway. With the top down, the sea's perfume floating in the wind, and Nat King Cole swinging smooth on the CD player, we do our best to decompress from a surreal and exhausting day. But as nuts as it was, I know I'm a lucky guy. I've got Candy Lou with me, driving with precision, checking the rearview mirror to make sure we're not being followed. Protecting me. I take a chance and touch her hand, hoping she doesn't brush it away. Time stops again as Nat does his best to assist me with his magic vocal cords. At last the unimaginable happens. Wrapping her fingers in mine, she brings my hand to her lips and kisses it tenderly. I look at my personal bodyguard—beautiful, confident, in control. She's ravishing, and most astonishingly, she actually likes me.

> *The shore was kissed*
> *By sea and mist, tenderly*
> *I can't forget*
> *How two hearts met*
> *breathlessly*

Back at my place, I whip up a can of ravioli while she checks the perimeter. Seriously, how many times does a guy get to say that in his lifetime? Later we sit in the backyard, drinking chardonnay and listening to the night sounds in the canyon. I don't want to think about Lal tonight. I don't want to think at all. With the grace of a dancer, Candy straddles my lap and we begin kissing and touching and pressing close, trying to keep the murderous energy of the outside world away by exploring the inner world of each other's bodies. We move together, protector and protectee, her gleaming eyes gazing into mine, an expression on her face that tells me I'm the one she'll take a bullet for. I'm the one who will never die on her watch. I'm the one she'll never lose.

> *Your arms opened wide*
> *And closed me inside*
> *You took my lips*
> *you took my love*
> *So tenderly.*

SIXTEEN   THE DOCTOR PAYS A CALL

HAVING MADE MY evening perfect, Candy accompanies me to the set and insists on getting my lunch for me, which has been laid out, buffet style, on Stage 16. She doesn't want me milling about when I don't absolutely have to, and she worries about the possibility of someone tampering with my food. Poisoning it. She thinks of everything. But she goes a little heavy on the vegetables, in my opinion. While waiting for her to return, I decided to engage in one of my famous ten-minute naps. I excel in the art of catching a little shut-eye.

I'm in my Data costume and makeup in the middle of a desert. Far in the distance, through waves of heat and blurry contacts, I can make out someone coming toward me. At first I think it's a mirage, or maybe Candy Lou coming back with my lunch. Then I see that the person is wearing a costume, too—that of Lal the genderless android! I start to panic and run away, up and over dunes, looking back to see Lal getting closer, never wavering. I can't seem to move any faster. My legs are so heavy. She's stronger than me.

My heart pounds. My lungs feel like they're on fire. I can't see through the contacts. I yell out: "Leave me alone, you're sick! Leave me the fuck alone!!!"

"Mr. Spiner, are you all right?" asks someone with a delicate English accent.

I open my eyes to see a gentle-looking bearded man gazing down at me, deep concern etched on his empathetic face. Ordinarily, I'd be frightened by the sudden appearance of a stranger in my trailer, but with the twinkle in his eyes and his snowy white whiskers, he resembles Edmund Gwenn as Kris Kringle in *Miracle on 34th Street*, a sort of Santa Claus in a brown tweed suit. Nothing scary about Santa Claus or brown tweed. I shake my head to clear the cobwebs from my brain.

"Yes, I'm okay, I was just having a nightmare, that's all. Actually, a daymare. Who are you?"

"My name is Oliver Sacks. I'm a neurologist. I'm visiting Paramount today because they're making a film based on a book of mine. But also, I very much wanted to meet you."

I feel instantly comfortable with him, which is unusual for me. I invite him to sit down and take a load off. "What's your book about, Doctor?" I inquire.

"It's about the victims of an encephalitis epidemic that began in the winter of 1916–17. The survivors were rendered catatonic. In my research, I discovered that using L-dopa medication stimulated a sort of 'awakening' in them. Robert De Niro is playing my primary patient, and Robin Williams is performing a version of me."

"Hmmm, impressive. But why did you want to meet me?"

I see it coming. He's about to offer me a role in the movie. Makes sense. Data. Catatonic. "Yada, yada, yada," as they say on Jerry Seinfeld's new show.

"Mr. Spiner, I have many patients with autism and Asperger's syndrome. They often have extreme difficulties with basic social interaction. For many of them, you or rather Data is their icon. Their hero."

I'm momentarily speechless, taking this in. "I'm not sure I understand."

"You see, Mr. Spiner—the inner world of a person with autism or Asperger's syndrome is very much like the feeling of being an emotionless android in a society of emotional humans. Like Data, they were born with a disability—they don't have an intuitive understanding of human feelings. It's a slow process of sometimes extremely difficult learning. But there can be results and change. So when they see what Data goes through, they relate to him. Relating to others offers self-esteem for them. He gives them self-esteem but also inspiration and hope. I even have a patient who has only one friend: Data. He can relate *only* to Data. In a way, you saved his life. You've touched people beyond the fan base, of which I am certainly a member."

This is so much more important than a role in a movie. This is significant. I feel overwhelmed with a combination of humility and self-importance, all at the same time.

"This is truly blowing my mind, Dr. Sacks. I had no idea about any of this. All I ever wanted to do was to entertain, but to think that I actually help people is really wonderful."

"Oh, you do, Mr. Spiner. In fact, I think of you as the poster boy for my work. You know, I have been said to suffer from Asperger's myself, but I think that overstates it. I'd say I'm an honorary Asperger. I'm also an honorary Tourette because I tend to jerk and occasionally I suddenly say something loud. And I'm an honorary bipolar. I suspect we all have a bit of everything inside of us."

"And obviously you're an honorary member of that group who doesn't knock before entering someone's private space," I joke.

"Indeed!" he says, laughing a little too loudly. "Anyway, I just wanted you to know, you are making a tremendous contribution to many of your fan's lives."

"Thank you, Doctor. I can't tell you how much that means to me."

Connection. Connection. These revelations of Dr. Sacks bring to mind the turmoil in my recent life. I think of Loretta's lurid fantasies. And of course I think of Lal.

"Dr. Sacks, have you ever heard of the Franklin Kurtz Mental Health Facility for Children in Duluth, Minnesota?" I ask.

"Oh yes, wonderful staff, beautiful campus. I've lectured there, but really that's the extent of my knowledge. I've never sent a patient there. We have more than enough long-term mental health facilities for young people in the tri-state area."

"But it's reputable? Legit?"

"Oh, by all means," he assures me.

There is an awkward moment of silence as Dr. Sacks and I regard each other. Perhaps we are both attempting to see the mysteries in us that lay beyond. Or maybe we've just run out of things to say.

Suddenly a blaring but familiar voice pierces the quiet. "Mr. Spiner! You in there?"

Oh no. I'm not ready for this.

"Yes, Detective Ortiz. Come on in."

Ortiz enters the trailer, a crocodile grin behind his moustache, his eyes bulging.

"Dr. Sacks, I'd like you to meet Detective Ortiz, head of obsessives at the LAPD."

"Head of obsessives? Oh my, that is intriguing," says Dr. Sacks without a hint of sarcasm.

"Mr. Spiner," says Ortiz, looking like he's about to explode, "I've got some great news for you!"

I bolt upright from the couch. "You found Lal?" My voice trembles in anticipation.

"Who?" asks Ortiz stupidly.

"Lal! My stalker!" I reply, practically screaming.

"Oh yeah. No, even better. Paramount is gonna produce my *Star Trek* spec script, the one where Data goes back in time and teams up with a Hispanic detective to solve a serial murder case! Apparently Roddenberry had a major hard-on for my writing!"

My mind is reeling. Did I give that script to any producers? I thought I threw it in the garbage!

"Your development guy, Mickey, told me you gave it to him to give to the higher-ups. Don't think I don't appreciate that. I owe you one, Mr. Spiner. Hey, what do you think about Tony Orlando, the singer, playing me? People say I look like him."

"Oh, I can't wait to see this," says Dr. Sacks. "I never miss an episode."

Dr. Oliver Sacks and Detective Ortiz begin a lively conversation about their favorite episodes of *Star Trek: The Next Generation*. If Rod Serling walked into my trailer right now and did an intro to a *Twilight Zone* episode, it wouldn't faze me at all. I lie back down on the couch, close my eyes, and do my best to tune them out. I'm almost certain I hear the word *massage,* but I force myself to ignore it as I drift back into dreamland.

SEVENTEEN   CHÂTEAU VIDEO

NIGHTTIME. PROBABLY SHOULDN'T have taken that nap earlier, but with my shooting schedule and with everything happening in my life, I find it impossible to keep a normal sleep schedule. This is one of those nights where I can't get my brain to turn off. So many thoughts. Candy wearing that Starfleet uniform. Candy taking off that Starfleet uniform. Stuff like that. Right now Candy is sleeping on the couch in the living room. She wanted to be in a different room from me, in the front of the house, should anything happen. If I keep thinking about her, I'll never get any sleep. I have to suppress my basic instinct to join her on that couch. Or on the floor. Or on the . . . STOP! I force myself to think of other things.

My thoughts drift to what Dr. Sacks said today, about my character helping people. I want to ponder this snippet of substance, because sometimes what I do for a living seems so foolish. I try to remember what made me want to do it in the first place. That first impulse. We lived in a two-story house in Houston when I was a child. I recall being at the top of the stairs and thinking about the movie we'd seen that afternoon: *Scared Stiff*, a haunted house comedy with Dean Martin and Jerry Lewis. I worshiped Jerry Lewis. "Hey, everyone," I said, "watch this!" I catapulted myself headfirst down the wooden stairway. When I reached the bottom, every inch of my body was screaming in pain. Totally unaware of my agony, my family burst into gales of laughter and enthusiastic applause. Somehow, I guess, that ovation caused my system to secrete some kind of endorphin, and the pain became irrelevant. I knew in that moment what I wanted to be. I wanted to make people laugh. I wanted to make them happy. But this feeling wasn't completely selfless. I didn't understand it at the time, but those laughs, that applause, represented approval. It made me feel worthwhile. Strange that all these years later, I still crave that drug. Dr. Sacks's revelation, however, arrives as a balm to my tortured soul. It comes without concern for my neurotic need for acceptance. After all, I wasn't even aware it was happening. It has a life of its own. And it moves me deeply that, even inadvertently, I've participated in making someone's life a little bit better.

For a moment, I'm able to relax, and sleep seems possible until my mind shifts to darker thoughts. Do I deserve what's happening to me? To be the object of someone's disturbed fantasy? Is this the price of dreams come true? I can't make sense of this Faustian bargain, and I don't want to. I just want it to be over. I want this person to be found and to leave me alone. I'm definitely not going to be able to sleep. As quietly as I can, I get dressed and slip out the back door. Candy will be upset that I stupidly risked going out without her, but she's been getting almost as little sleep as I have and I don't have the heart to wake her. I need to watch a movie, and though my local video store is only three blocks away, I take my car. With the doors locked and the windows up, I feel almost invincible. Almost. When I enter the store, aptly called Château Video, there's no one behind the counter. I hear Perry Como singing:

> *Somebody up there likes me,*
> *Somebody up there cares!*
> *Somebody up there knows my fears,*
> *And hears my silent prayers!*

A black-and-white movie is playing on the store TV monitors. The Brooklyn Bridge very late at night, the black-and-white contrast so stark, it feels like opposites attracting. I know this movie well. *Somebody Up There Likes Me* with Paul Newman, Pier Angeli, and Sal Mineo. Came out in 1956. I was about seven. I saw it three times in one day. The first time, my day-care counselor, Bob, took me and the rest of the kids in my group to the ten o'clock morning show. He parked us in the first three rows, then disappeared into the balcony with his girlfriend until the movie was over. The other kids grew bored and threw popcorn and Milk Duds at each other, but I was transfixed. There was something about this movie. Later, I convinced my mother to let me go with our next-door neighbors, who were taking in an afternoon showing. And that evening after supper, we went on a family outing to the movies. My stepfather was pushing for *Battle Cry* with Aldo Ray, but my mother didn't think it was appropriate for kids. She wanted to see the Paul Newman movie, though it was also probably not appropriate for kids, and that afforded me my third viewing of the day.

Watching the TV monitors in the video store, I realize that I haven't seen this movie since that day. And yet I recall perfectly the scenes of a young boy being given boxing lessons by his brutish father. The man wears a wifebeater undershirt just as my stepfather did, and shouts at the boy. "Come on, fight me back, come on!" He punches the son in the face and knocks him down. Blood drips from the boy's nose. "I don't like crybabies," the father says. I recall being hypnotized by this father/son dynamic and how I saw myself in that boy. I wonder if my stepfather saw himself in the father character as he watched the film. Probably not. Though he never struck me with his fist, only a belt or a board, his lessons were equally severe. I never saw the fathers of my friends lay a hand on them. Until I saw this movie, I thought it was only me and my brother who suffered this indignity. And I no longer felt that we were alone. Suddenly my thoughts go to the kids that Dr. Sacks spoke about, how they see themselves in Data. "I suspect we all have a bit of everything inside of us," he said. Indeed, Dr. Sacks. Indeed.

The owner of the store, Jeff, comes out of a back room

and greets me like an old friend. "Hey, Brent. What'll it be tonight?"

"I don't know, let me look around," I reply, gravitating to the thriller section.

Browsing through the available films, I take one from the shelf, something called *The Fan*. I read the description on the back of the VHS box: "Lauren Bacall is a Broadway actress terrorized by a dangerous fan who becomes enraged when his letters are ignored by her." Sounds interesting, even though I'm not crazy about Bacall. Realizing this film may be a little close to home, I nonetheless consider it research. Maybe there's something in it that will give me more insight into my own dilemma. Ironically, and tragically, this movie was released just months after John Lennon was murdered by an obsessive Beatles fan, Mark David Chapman, who also thought he was a character in *Catcher in the Rye*.

"Oh, hey," Jeff calls out, "your wife came in again today. Mrs. Spiner."

That stops me cold. "What?"

"Yeah, she's come in every day for the last week. Calls herself Mrs. Spiner. Nice person. A little weird. She said that she moved here from the East Coast because she needed more 'Brent time.'"

I feel a chill crawling up the back of my neck. "Wait a minute . . . what are you talking about?" I ask.

"I kid you not," he says. "Somehow she knows this is where you rent your videos. I guess she's hoping to run into you here. Oh, she also bought a season of *Star Trek: The Next Generation.*"

"She did?" I ask warily. "Was it the season with 'The Offspring' in it?"

He checks his log. "No, she bought season two. 'The Offspring' is in season three."

My mind is spinning. What the hell is happening here?

"Can you describe what she looks like?"

He thinks a moment then offers his professional opinion. "She kind of looks like Jodie Foster. Not *Taxi Driver* Jodie. More like . . ."

He points to a poster on the wall of *Silence of the Lambs.* I look at Jodie Foster's face on the poster. Her mouth is covered by a large moth. On the moth's back is a tiny skull. I flash back to John Hinckley. A mega-crazy fan of Jodie Foster's who shot Reagan to impress her. Jesus, to impress her. My mind can't handle this. Not tonight. Why did I come here without Candy? I need a diversion.

"Do you have any Laurel and Hardy?" I inquire.

Taking my bag of videos with me, I head out of the store, and into the night. MRS. SPINER??? Though it's only a couple of blocks drive home, I can't make it. I pull over to the side of the road and vomit into someone's bougainvillea. Mrs. Spiner, who resembles Jodie Foster, which is also what Cindy Lou looks like and by extension Candy, albeit with darker hair. Is Mrs. Spiner Lal? Is this Loretta? Has she come to Los Angeles? I've got to call Cindy Lou first thing in the morning.

She needs to know about this. And I need to know what in the world is going on.

Parking my car in the driveway, I tiptoe through the yard to the back door. I slip the key into the lock as quietly as I can so as not wake Candy. Just as I turn the doorknob to let myself in, an arm comes from behind me and locks around my neck. As my muscles tighten, a series of hormones shoot through my body, my heart beating like a Buddy Rich drum solo. I open my mouth to scream, but nothing comes out. Then I'm forcefully whirled around and I find myself eyeball-to-eyeball with Candy. She's not wearing her happy face.

"Don't you ever sneak out like that again!" she spits through clenched teeth.

"Jesus Christ, Candy, you scared the shit out of me!" I say, finally managing to activate my vocal chords.

"Listen, mister," she says, her index finger in my face, "I'm here primarily to do my job. I can't do that if you behave like an idiot. I was frantic. How was I supposed to know what happened to you?"

"I'm sorry. I couldn't sleep and I didn't want to wake you. You looked so sweet—"

"Maybe . . ." she interrupts, "we should keep this strictly professional?"

Neither one of us moves for what seems like an eternity. Finally, like magnets, a vital force pulls us together and we grab ahold of each other like there's no tomorrow. And truthfully, there's every possibility there may not be.

"Can we talk about it in the morning?" I ask hopefully.

"Where the hell did you go?" she says, not answering my question.

Disengaging from our embrace, I hold up the plastic bag containing the fruits of my mission. "I got movies. Do you like Laurel and Hardy?"

This question is more important to me than anyone can possibly imagine. I've always been of a mind that I couldn't trust anyone who didn't like Laurel and Hardy.

"Are you kidding?" she asked, looking at me like I'd lost my marbles. "Do I like Laurel and Hardy? Are you out of your mind?"

"Well, I just wanted to—"

"Do I like Laurel and Hardy?" she says again. "I fucking *love* Laurel and Hardy."

We melt together, becoming one mind, one body. The evening has taken an unexpected but decidedly upward turn. We make our way to the bedroom, where we pop in a tape and giggle our way through Stan and Ollie's dance routine in *Way Out West*. Not to be outdone, we choreograph a dance of our own, so to speak. And we do our best to perfect it. All through the night and into the morning.

EIGHTEEN   A GUN IN THE FIRST ACT

BLESSEDLY, I HAVE a noon set call. Gives me time to get a jump on my lines before I go. I only have a couple of short scenes, which is a good thing. My legs are a little wobbly from last night's tango.

Though I assumed Candy would be coming with me, she convinces me that there's ample security on the Paramount lot and that if I stick to my trailer, only leaving to go to set and shoot scenes, I should be fine. She feels that if Mrs. Spiner knows where I get my videos, there's a good chance she also knows where I live and my schedule, and could very well show up at my house when she thinks I've gone to work.

"I want to be here if she makes that mistake," says Candy.

"Are you sure you'll be okay by yourself?" I ask. "I mean, she could be Lal."

"With any luck at all, she will be Lal, and then this mystery will be solved. No, it's better if I'm alone. I have some inter-rogation tactics that I'd rather you not see. Not yet, anyway."

The corners of her mouth turn upward into that bewitching smile, and I find myself both frightened and a little turned on. In fact, a lot turned on. Shake it off. I gotta go to work.

I live a short eight minutes from the studio, door to door. A straight drive down Camrose, then Highland to the Hollywood Freeway, Gower exit to Melrose, and into the lot. I enjoy that drive. Gives me a few minutes to become one with the real world before going into outer space. Sort of like a brief meditation. Much as I love the company of Candy Lou, it feels good to be alone in my car. I'm one of those people who really need alone time. And I think I'm actually getting stronger. I might even be able to handle this stalker thing without a bodyguard. Maybe Candy and I could drop that aspect of our relationship and just date. Then, it crosses my mind that if Mrs. Spiner knows where I live and knows my schedule, she probably knows my car. What if she's following me? I swivel my head from side to side, checking my rearview and side-view mirrors to see if anything unusual is happening around me. Everything seems okay for the moment, aside from a crick in my neck, but I still wish Candy was sitting next to me. Forget what I said about dropping the bodyguard part.

The entrance into the studio is pretty standard. A guard gate divides the road, occupied by one or two security officers. A black-and-white-striped barrier blocks your access until they check your identity, after which they raise it, allowing you to drive onto the lot. I pull up to the booth, where I'm greeted by the morning security guard, Rudy. Rudy has greeted me every day since I started on the show. He's pretty much a fixture at the studio, having worked there as long as anyone can remember. He still speaks fondly of Rudolph Valentino.

"Good morning, Mr. Spiner!" he booms in his typical happy-to-be-here way.

"Morning, Rudy. Say, uh, has anyone unusual come to the gate in the last couple hours? Anyone wanting to come to the *Star Trek* set? To see me?"

"Well, now you mention it, yeah. A woman came by this morning on foot, but not to see you. Said she was Wil Wheaton's tutor. I called the office to see if they had her on the list but turns out the kid's not even working today. She said she must've gotten the day wrong and walked off down Melrose."

"Do you remember what she looked like?" I ask.

"Yeah, she was blond. Looked kind of like that actress . . ."

"Jodie Foster?" I offered.

"No, no, not her. The one who did that picture with Kirk Douglas's boy. *Fatal Attraction*. You know, the one with a man's name."

"Glenn Close?"

"Yeah! That's her. Dead ringer."

I release a deep sigh, relieved that I won't be meeting Mrs. Spiner today.

"Glenn . . . funny name for a woman. You know, Glenn Ford shot a few pictures here. You wouldn't believe it, but Glenn Ford laid more pipe than any man in Hollywood. Him and Kirk, the ladies loved them. I was here when Kirk and Burt Lancaster shot *Gunfight at the O.K. Corral* on the back lot," Rudy continues. "Burt was a hell of a nice guy. Kirk, he was a prick. But I'm told that since he survived that copter crash, he's become a sweetheart. Guess a near-death experience brings out the best in a person."

Much as I want to stay and listen to more of Rudy's reminiscences, if I dawdle any longer, I'm going to be late. I bid him a good day and drive to the tank, as it's known, to park my car. The tank is a huge hole in the ground that, when not used as a parking lot, can be filled with hundreds of gallons of water. Cecil B. DeMille shot the parting of the Red Sea in that very tank. At least that's what they say.

Dashing across the lot to the hair and makeup trailer, I pass Gerri, my favorite production assistant. "Gerri, could you grab my contacts and bring them to makeup, please?"

"Sure," she shouts over her shoulder. "Hey, I think I can still get you breakfast. The usual?"

My usual breakfast at the studio is a feast of twelve dollar-sized pancakes smothered in butter and syrup and three orders of bacon, well done. I'll worry about my heart later in life. But since my introduction to a pig's penis, I can't really stomach pork anymore.

"Just the cakes today, thanks."

I hop into the makeup trailer and slide into one of the available chairs. Dorn is there getting the finishing touches added to the ridged prosthetic glued to his forehead. As usual, his concentration is focused on the daily *New York Times* crossword puzzle.

"Hey, Dorny! I've got a favor to ask you."

He is oblivious to me and continues with his task of solving 27 across.

"I've got a neighbor, couple of houses down, and he has this gerbil. Cute little thing. And he just loves it. That's his idea of a pet. I don't get it, but anyway, the gerbil has suddenly stopped eating. The guy is just despondent. He's so upset, he can't eat, either."

I can almost see the invisible steam shooting from Dorn's ears.

"So I was wondering if you do house calls? Maybe you could stop by and give the gerbil the benefit of your veterinary—"

"Brent," he interrupts, "don't make me get out of this chair and come hurt you."

I love fucking with Dorn.

A moment later Gerri pops in and hands me my contacts. "Here you go, Brent. Oh, also, Mickey just dropped your mail, so I grabbed that for you, too," she says, putting a few letters on the counter in front of me.

"Three! Three lousy letters?" I say, certain there's been a mistake. I turn to Gates, who is sitting in the makeup chair next to mine having her gorgeous red locks blown out.

"Gates!" I shout over the annoying whir of the hair dryer, "how much fan mail did you get this week?"

"I don't know," she shouts back. "About half a bucket full, I guess."

Better to keep my disappointment to myself. I silently console myself with the thought that there must be a sorting problem in the mailroom. Flipping through my measly take, I spot Loretta's familiar return address. But, oddly, the name above the address is Andrew Gibson. Uh-oh. Reluctantly I open it.

Brent Spiner,

I am Loretta Gibson's husband. I just came home from the road and found my wife writing a letter to you. You better leave my wife alone. She's not like you Hollywood people who can handle these kinds of racy affairs. I gave her a gun years ago because I'm away so much, so you really don't want to mess with this woman's heart. Take it from me. She doesn't like being played the fool. And neither do I. She's had a hard time adjusting to our new living situation, and she's very fragile right now. Just leave her alone and stop calling. You don't want to mess with her and you sure as hell don't want to mess with me. If this doesn't stop immediately, I will call the authorities.

Andrew Gibson

Great. Just what I need, an enraged husband. This guy thinks he has a problem with me? His problem is much more serious than he thinks. Either his wife is a dangerous stalker or she has just completely lost her mind. Or both.

When I get back to my trailer, I call Cindy Lou Jones.

"This is Agent Jones," she answers

"Agent Jones. Cindy Lou, where have you been?"

"Are you asking me that question in an official capacity?" she asks, like the good FBI agent she is.

"What else?" I say in an official capacity.

"I've been in beautiful Dull-uth, Minnesota, trying to track down your stalker, Mr. Spiner."

"What? Why didn't you tell me you were going to Duluth?"

"FBI procedure. We're not allowed to offer any information on a case unless you directly ask us."

"Okay, so what happened?"

"I'll fill you in when I see you. My sister says there's a new note from Lal that you received at a convention. I'd like to take possession of that."

"Yes, I have it here someplace."

I pick up my jacket and rifle through the pockets, finally locating the note handed to me by Data Jr. in San Diego. In the process, I leave golden handprints all over what was previously a perfectly nice windbreaker.

"I'll come by as soon as I can," she says, hanging up.

I find myself reading Lal's letter again. One part jumps out at me, and I can feel the muscles in my jaws tightening. "By the way, I'm really sorry about Uncle Trey. I saw him last night and he said to tell you to stop messing with his wife." Jesus Christ. I shudder. How dare she mention Trey or his wife! And how does she know about him? That he died? Did she listen to the phone call I had with my mother? Are my phones tapped? A knock at the door snaps me out of my thoughts. I look through the window and spy Agent Cindy Lou Jones, in the flesh, back from the wilds of Duluth, Minnesota. Seeing her, I'm again stunned by how identical she and Candy are in appearance. Except for the hair and the carriage, they're practically indistinguishable.

I open the door. "That was fast," I say.

"I was on the lot," she replies, flashing that enchanting Cindy/Candy smile. "There's a VIP on set today. I needed to secure it and lock it down. Good to see you alive, Mr. Spiner."

"Good to be alive, Agent Jones. Come in."

I gesture for Cindy Lou to come inside and take a seat. I'm not sure why, but I close the door behind her and lock it. I suppose I don't want anyone disturbing us.

"A lot has happened since we last spoke," I share, handing her the note from Lal. "And I just received this today from Loretta Gibson's husband, Andrew."

She takes the Andrew Gibson letter and after reading it, surmises: "This Loretta Gibson is clearly suffering from erotomania, the delusion that the two of you are infatuated with each other and are having an affair. Albeit over the phone. And either her husband is also convinced of this or she could have written this letter herself."

"Right!" I agree. "I never thought of that. That's really smart. Or maybe she's Lal? I don't know, it's so confusing."

"Don't worry, Mr. Spiner. We're going to clear all this up, I promise."

"I didn't know the FBI made promises. Or that they make promises only when you *ask* them to make promises," I tease.

"That's my personal promise to you," she purrs in that sexy forties voice.

Something about that voice makes me want to believe her.

"So, give it up. What did you find out in Duluth?" I ask.

She pulls out a spiral pad and refers to her notes. "I met

with the director of the facility, Dr. Sandra Ogilvy. She was very helpful. She has a patient named Grace, who suffers from paranoid personality disorder. Seems she has a major obsession with your character, Data. Dr. Ogilvy had never seen the show, so they watched a few episodes together in the common room at the facility. She wanted to understand what Data means to Grace and hopefully help her to loosen the obsession and ultimately let it go. She felt they were making progress when Grace ran away about a week ago."

I start to break out in what I hope is not a noticeable sweat. But as the gold makeup starts running down my face, I know the jig is up.

"Well, do you have any leads? Has she contacted anyone?" I ask, dabbing at my chin with a tissue.

"Grace's parents run a fishing resort in Lake Winnibigosh-ish, southeast of Minneapolis. I spoke to them on the phone. They haven't heard from Grace and she hasn't been home. I sent one of my guys to go have a meet and greet with them. I didn't go myself because I have a gut feeling they were telling the truth. The doctor said she wasn't close to them. She also said that in her last session with her, the girl was highly agitated. This suggests to me that she would look for comfort to soothe her anxieties, and clearly her family doesn't provide that. They don't seem particularly involved in her life, having sent her away when she was fifteen. They don't know who her friends are, or even if she has any. It's possible she could have made her way to San Diego, and she could even be here in Los Angeles right now. We just don't know yet."

"Well, you've gotta find her and take her back to that mental facility," I say, gold droplets starting to dot my uniform.

"I understand," she offers sympathetically, "but that's a bit of a problem. The Franklin Kurtz Mental Health Facility is only for juveniles. Grace turned eighteen three days after she left. They can't legally treat her any longer. As it was, they were only days away from having to release her."

"This just keeps getting better and better." I belch, with a combination of irony and agita.

This morning's pancakes start moving back up to my mouth as I think about this new twist. Cindy Lou's attention turns to the VHS tapes on my couch of *The Fan* and the Laurel and Hardy compilations that I plan on dropping off after work.

"*The Fan*? Are you having a stalker film festival, Mr. Spiner?"

"Not really. I just thought it might help me understand the psychology of what's going on. And then the Laurel and Hardy was meant to help me forget what's going on. Do you like Laurel and Hardy?"

I submit that question wondering what kind of future we might have.

"Did you learn anything from *The Fan*?" Cindy Lou asks, ignoring me.

"I didn't have time to watch it. I was . . . busy," I say, avoiding telling her what I was busy doing.

"Too bad. It's actually quite germane to what's been happening to you. A creepy fan is obsessed with a stage and film star. TV, in your case."

"Hey, I've worked on stage and in films," I counter superficially.

"Of course you have," she says, placating me. "Anyway, he sends her letters professing his adoration for her and begins stalking her. He becomes inflamed when he sees her responses as cold and concludes that they're probably written by someone else. His sense of self-esteem is based on his feelings of connection to the celebrity. The more connection he has, the more powerful he feels, the more he likes himself. And the less connection, the more he hates himself. And in turn, the more he hates the celebrity. In the end, well, I don't want to spoil it for you."

"Go ahead, tell me what hap—"

"It's celebrity versus stalker in a bloody fight to the death," she reveals. "Sorry. You asked."

"Is this where my life is headed, Agent Jones? Toward a bloody fight to the death?"

I'm perspiring so much that I'm dangerously close to needing my makeup completely redone.

"Don't worry, Brent," says Cindy Lou. "I won't let anything happen to you."

Jesus, that's exactly what Candy said to me. As I hear the same words come out of the same face, it's almost like déjà vu. Except it actually happened.

"So . . . are you saying this girl, Grace, wants to hu-hurt me?" I stutter.

"We can't be absolutely certain that Grace is sending the letters. It's a solid lead, but we don't have the evidence.

"Right. Oh, there's something I haven't mentioned yet. When I was getting these movies, the video store owner told me there's a woman coming in who calls herself Mrs. Spiner. Said she just moved to L.A. for more 'Brent time' and that she looks just like Jodie Foster. Could that be Grace?"

Agent Jones logs this new information in her notepad. "I doubt it. Probably someone entirely different. Dr. Ogilvy described Grace as stocky with straight black hair. Long. Doesn't sound much like Jodie Foster. Funny, people tell me I look like Jodie Foster. I get that a lot since *Silence of the Lambs* came out."

I had that exact thought the first time I saw her. Now I'm having other thoughts. Thoughts I'm afraid to say out loud, and yet . . .

"I know this is a crazy thing for me to ask you, but, Agent Jones . . . are you Mrs. Spiner?"

Again, she flashes that Cindy/Candy smile. Only this time there's something mysterious in it. "No, Mr. Spiner, I'm not. Not yet, anyway."

I sink into the chair behind me. I don't know what to make of that. And I don't know how to respond. Finally . . .

"That was a joke," she says.

"Oh . . . ha!" I laugh unconvincingly.

"Nonetheless," she continues, leaning toward me, "why don't we lay our cards on the table?"

"Do you mean that in a . . . professional capacity?" I burble.

"I know you slept with my sister."

Okay, now my head is whirling so rapidly, it might actually disengage from my neck. "I did?" I ask lamely.

"Yes, Mr. Spiner, you did. She briefed me all about it. Or should I say, taunted me?"

"Taunted you?"

"When I asked her to be your bodyguard, I made it very clear to her that I was attracted to you from the moment I met you. I should've known she'd make a play for you. We can be very competitive. After all, we're like two sides of the same coin."

Talk about shocking disclosures. From the moment she met me? This never happens to me. Usually, I have to dazzle with my rapier wit or my insincere humility. And even then, it's rare that anyone's interested.

"Well, I . . . I'm flattered, to say the least. This is getting really complicated."

"I thought you should know," she says, touching my hand. "Why don't we talk more about it another time. I'm still on the clock."

"Okay, Candy."

"Cindy."

"Right! Sorry . . . I . . ."

"Don't worry about it. People have made that mistake before. I'm going to run checks on this Andrew Gibson. And talk to your video guy. But I'll see you at the VIP meeting later."

"Oh yeah," I say, remembering, "who's coming?"

"It's a surprise," she answers, putting her finger to her lips. She goes to the door and unlocks it.

As she's about to leave, I stop her. "By the way . . . which side of the coin are you? Heads or tails?"

"Oh, I can be either," she teases. "Depending on the situation, of course."

The woman definitely knows how to make an exit. I sit alone in my trailer pondering the tangled web of my life. Someone wants to kill me. Someone wants to leave her husband for me because she thinks I'm calling her and talking dirty to her. Someone has moved to California and thinks she's married to me. And now I'm romantically in the grips of twin law enforcement officers. I suppose my fate could be much worse. Not weirder, but probably worse. I gotta get my makeup redone and get into a fresh space suit.

NINETEEN DUTCH ON STAGE SIXTEEN

AFTER A COUPLE of scenes in Engineering with LeVar and Dorn, I clean myself up as best I can and head to Stage 16, where we've been instructed to gather for a very special visit. Stage 16 is a swing stage that transforms into various other planets when called for. I once tried to add a clause into my contract that I'd get a bonus whenever my feet touched the surface of another planet. The studio wouldn't bite. Currently, Stage 16 is dressed with the mountains of Atalia VII, wherever the hell that is. Gene Roddenberry is sitting in a tall director's chair, his cane balanced between his legs. Patrick, Rick Berman, and the rest of the cast and crew working today gather in groups, schmoozing in anticipation of the big moment. The stage door opens and in bursts—literally *bursts*—none other than Ronald Reagan. He looks fantastic. Better than on television. Wearing a perfectly tailored brown suit, he is taller than expected and shockingly handsome. As Gene rises to greet him, his cane falls to the floor. In his present physical condition, there is no possible way he can bend over and retrieve it. Without breaking his stride, Reagan swoops down, snatches up the cane, and offers it to Gene in one graceful uninterrupted move. Fred Astaire couldn't have done it better. Impressive as it is, one can't help being struck by the fact that Reagan is ten years Gene's senior. Life has many ways of being unfair, and none crueler than the limits imposed by each individual's genetics. Accompanying Reagan are three FBI agents, including one Cindy Lou Jones, who in her professional mode does her best not to make eye contact with me. At the former president's side is his best friend, A. C. Lyles, a dapper gentleman known to many as the goodwill ambassador of Paramount. A. C.'s history at the studio reaches back almost as far as that of Rudy, the gate guard. Just out of college, he became office boy for one of Paramount's founders, Adolph Zukor. In a short time, he graduated to publicity, and eventually produced low-budget Westerns. Those films were said to have saved the studio when it was going through difficult financial times. Ironically, many of them starred DeForest Kelley, Bones of *Star Trek* fame.

"You know . . ." says Ronald Reagan, gazing around the set, "I've always wondered what would happen if there was a real alien invasion of planet Earth."

"That's what *Star Trek*'s about, Ronnie," encourages A. C.

"Perhaps we humans need some outside universal threat to make us recognize our common bond. Sometimes I think how quickly our differences worldwide would vanish if we were facing an alien threat from outside this world."

"Indeed," says Patrick. "And it would be fascinating to know *why* the aliens are threatening Earth in your hypothetical scenario. Empathy is the key to understanding aggression."

Reagan gazes at Patrick. "Well, I don't know about that . . ."

Suddenly A. C. Lyles jumps in and begins introducing us. "Ron, I'd like you to meet Brent Spiner. He plays Lieutenant Commander Data on the show." Reagan shakes my hand vigorously. Much as I was not an advocate of his administration, I have to admit, it's kind of thrilling to meet him. After all, he was a part of my childhood. I was a devotee of the series, *Death Valley Days,* which he hosted in the mid-fifties, when he was just Ronald Reagan, the actor and borax soap peddler.

"I know you. The robot. Pretending to be a human."

Good God, he watches the show. I wonder if Nancy watches with him? Nah.

"Well, sir, my character doesn't actually pretend to be a human, he—"

A. C. interrupts, coming to the rescue of both of us. "How does it feel to be back at Paramount, Ronny?"

Reagan takes a wistful look around the stage. "Like coming home, again," he replies. "I did most of my pictures at Warner Bros., but I did three pictures here. So I guess you could say, more like a vacation home."

We all laugh a little too hard. I mean, what the fuck, it's Ronald Reagan.

"What films were those, Mr. President?" asks Rick Berman, as big a movie buff as I am.

A strange look appears in Reagan's eyes, almost as if he heard the question and yet didn't. After an awkward pause, things seem to snap into focus. "Well, I don't really recall the names of the pictures," he says in that familiar Reagan voice. "But I do know they all costarred lovely Rhonda Fleming."

"That's right, Ronnie! The Queen of Technicolor!" pipes up A. C.

Reagan scans the room again, landing at last on Agent Cindy Lou Jones. "You've got a good face for the movies, young lady," he says to her. "Maybe if you colored your hair red, like Rhonda, you could be a star."

She lowers her head, slightly embarrassed, and responds. "Thank you, Mr. President. That's very kind of you. And I'd like to say that if I'd been there that day, I'd have taken that bullet for you."

That strange look comes into his eyes again. But I can guarantee it is no stranger than the look in mine. What did she just say?

After the meet and greet with President Reagan ends, everyone disperses, and I head for the parking lot. On my way out, I decide to stop at LeVar's trailer. I stick my head in the door. "Hey, Burt, you still here?"

He calls out from the bathroom at the back of the trailer. "Yeah, Spine! Take a seat, I'm just having a pee."

A few seconds later, he emerges and lights about a dozen sticks of incense and a few candles.

"You planning to stay for a while?" I inquire.

"No, I'm leaving in a couple of minutes. I like to get centered before I hit the road."

He really takes this shit seriously. But then, he is more in touch with the cosmos than anyone I know. Which explains why I'm here.

"Burt, can I ask you a hypothetical question?"

"My favorite kind," he says, rubbing lavender oil into his hands.

It's difficult to gather my thoughts, but I take a deep breath and plunge in. "Say there's this guy and he's having an affair with this woman. Incredible woman. And she has a twin sister, equally incredible. It seems like the sister is sort of coming on to him. And, crazy as he is about the first one, he finds the other one just as intriguing, in a different way."

"All right, let's cut the bullshit, shall we? You're having trouble keeping up with the Joneses, right?

"Right," I admit. "But it's even more than that. There are times, Burt, I'd swear they're the same person. Except for a couple of superficialities, and the color of their hair, they're practically identical."

LeVar looks at me with a sad expression on his face. "They're twins."

"I know, I know, but they look at me the same way. They smile the same way. They say the same things and have the same vernacular."

"Twins do that, Spine. They grew up together and spent their whole lives together. Listen, you've gotta get ahold of yourself. Don't you have enough going on without this?"

"I know you're right, but I've never met anyone like . . . them."

LeVar widens his extra large eyes and attempts to bore a hole into my brain.

"Spine, look at me. There are two sisters. And you can't have both of them. Well, you can, but believe me, you'll pay for it."

"Yeah, I'm sure that's true," I say, not absolutely convinced. "I must've done something in a past life that I'm paying for now."

"Well, if you want to see someone, I know a guy who specializes in past life regression."

As I'm about to politely refuse, Jonathan steps into the trailer. "Hey, sorry to break up the party, but I thought you'd want to see this. This was in Genie's fan mail." He hands me a letter. This time, it's clumsily typewritten.

> *Dear Genie Francis,*
>
> *I thought you should know a couple of things. First, I never watch* General Hospital *anymore. It sucks since Demi Moore left the show. I much prefer* One Life to Live. *And I also wanted you to know that your husband, Commander Riker, is having a very steamy affair with Commander Data.*
> *Here's a condom for you.*
>
> *Data's loving daughter,*
> *Lal*

It's funny, but it's not.

Jonathan suggests that since it's still early we go for a quick bite before heading home. Hanging out with my pals sounds good. I've missed that. But LeVar has an appointment with an astral projection coach, so Johnny and I are on our own. I make a quick call to Candy to make sure she doesn't mind staying at the house alone for a little longer.

"Hi. Anything happen today? No unwanted guests?"

"Nope. Nothing. Been quiet all day." she says with a hint of disappointment.

"Good. Listen, Jonathan is having some personal issues he needs to talk to me about. Do you mind if I grab a drink or something with him before I come home?"

We've been intimate for only a short time and I'm already lying to her. I'm such a coward where women are concerned.

"No problem," she says. "I'm going to take a bath and relax. Maybe clean my gun. I'll see you when you get home."

She's so great. I probably should've just told her the truth. Now the guilt kicks in.

"Okay, I won't be late. I'll bring you something to eat," I say, trying to make myself feel better.

"Just be cautious. Be aware. I don't want anything happening to you."

We decide that taking Jonathan's car might be a good misdirection. It's a safer bet that no one will follow him.

"Where shall we go?" I ask.

"Have you ever been to Chasen's? That's where the big players go."

Chasen's is a famous restaurant in Hollywood, bordering Beverly Hills, which has been operating since 1936. It's been frequented over the years by the crème de la crème of show business. Frank Sinatra, Cary Grant, Jimmy Stewart, Cagney, Gable, you name it. Some stars even had their own booth named after them. After leaving the car with the valet, we walk into what strikes me as a Tinseltown Shangri-la. It's overwhelming. I swear, the music from *Lost Horizon* is playing in my head. Famous faces are everywhere, including the ghosts of years gone by. Jesus, this is the place where Orson Welles threw a can of flaming Sterno at John Houseman. We spot the brilliant director Billy Wilder deep in conversation with Jack Lemmon in the front booth, and I know I'm in the right place.

"Good choice, Johnny." I say as I scan the room with bulging eyes.

The maître d' shows us to our own red leather booth and seats us.

"Was this anyone's booth in particular?" I ask.

"Still is," he answers. "This is the Ronald Reagan Booth."

Jonathan and I shoot each other a look.

"Serendipity." He winks.

We order a couple of martinis and a gargantuan seafood platter, which looks large enough to have emptied the Pacific Ocean. Maybe I'll take some oysters home to Candy. Wink wink. Christ, did I just think that?

"So is the FBI getting any closer to solving this stalker thing?" asks Jonathan, sucking on a crab leg the size of my foot.

"Johnny, don't let's talk about that tonight. Let's just enjoy the drinks and the room and the vibe and thank our lucky stars that we're here."

At that instant, a rumbling, rolling sensation begins undulating from the floor as the walls begin to shake, glasses break, chandeliers rock back and forth, and a few tchotchkes tumble from a shelf above us. We grab the edges of the table and hold on for dear life. And then it stops. Everyone looks around and laughs in that uncomfortable way they do when they've just been through a minor earthquake and know they're going to live. I feel like singing "San Francisco" à la Jeanette MacDonald in the movie of the same name, but my good sense tells me that no one would think it was funny. Or for that matter, even get the reference. And then I see him. Sitting at a table across the room, unperturbed by the tremors, dining on a butterflied steak and a tomato and onion salad, is none other than Gregory Peck. Gregory fucking Peck!

"Johnny, try to be cool, but take a look behind you at the table in the corner."

"Wow, I love Gregory Peck."

"Yeah, me too. He's one of my favorites. I think I should go over there and tell him how much he's meant to me."

"Don't. He's obviously enjoying a quiet dinner with his wife. Didn't you just tell me to be cool?"

He's right. But I can't take my eyes off him. A couple of minutes later Peck excuses himself and disappears into the men's room.

"Ooh, I drank too much coffee at work today," I use as an excuse. "I'll be right back."

When I sidle up to the urinal next to Peck, he's just shaking off the last few drops from his member and zipping up. I look over to him and the stupidest words possible come out of my grinning face.

"Nice shake," I say, referring to the earthquake we just shared.

He obviously misinterprets my meaning, and a look of horror and disgust furrows his granite brow. Rapidly washing his hands, he rushes past me and out the door.

"You dumb, stupid fuck!" I say to my reflection in the mirror.

When I return to our booth, I look over to his table, and see that Mr. Peck is miming the universal sign for the check.

"Johnny, let's get the check."

"What? We still have half of this seafood tower left."

"I really need to get home. I'll ask them to split it into doggie bags."

To Jonathan's displeasure, I wave for the check, and we manage to make it outside, doggie bags in hand, just in time for the valet to pull up in Peck's Jaguar.

As he chivalrously opens the door for his wife and crosses around his car to fetch the keys from the valet, I make my move.

"Excuse me, Mr. Peck. I'm so sorry, but I feel it necessary to explain. In the men's room when I said *shake,* I was talking about the earthquake, not your . . . your . . ." I say, gesturing at his fly.

"Young man," he interrupts, "I'd like to have a nice private evening with my wife, if you don't mind."

"No, no, please, I totally understand. I'm an actor, too. It happens to me all the time!"

He narrows his eyes, gives me one last once-over, without the least glimmer of recognition, hops into his Jag, and speeds away.

By this time, Jonathan is so put off he can barely look at me. On the way home, he finally opens up. "Of all people, you should know better than that."

"I know. I'm so embarrassed. I couldn't help myself. I just wanted him to know how much I love him. Maybe I should drop him a note?"

He gives me an ironic look, the raised eyebrow kind. I guess I understand what it means to be a fan. I'm one, too, just like everyone else. Except Lal, of course. That's different. Johnny drops me at my car and I head off to return the tapes I rented at the video store before going home. Oh shit, I forgot the to-go bag for Candy in Jonathan's car.

TWENTY   THE BIG GOODBYE

PULLING INTO THE parking lot of Château Video, I put my hazards on and leave the motor running, planning to be there for just a few seconds. Jeff, the manager, is at the counter watching the movie *Laura* on the monitors. *Laura* is the story of a beautiful young woman who is murdered. Then it turns out she is not dead at all. Mistaken identity. And thus, the mystery begins. Jeff sees me come in and the googly look on his face, watching Gene Tierney and Dana Andrews fall in love, fades and becomes dour and serious.

"Brent, there's something I need to tell you. The woman who called herself Mrs. Spiner—"

"Yeah?" I say tentatively, growing anxious at the change in his demeanor.

"She was hit by a car crossing the street at Hollywood and Vine. Paramedics took her to the hospital on Vermont. She . . . didn't make it."

Another in what seems an endless series of gut punches.

Whoever she was, she moved to L.A. to be near me, a person she didn't even know. And now she's dead.

"A couple of friends from her acting class came in and brought back the tapes she'd rented. All *Star Trek* films. They told me about what happened, so I didn't charge them a late fee. The class is having a celebration of her life at First Presbyterian Church on Gower Street tomorrow evening."

"What about the driver?" I mumble. "Did the police talk to them?"

"No. It was a hit-and-run."

Was "Mrs. Spiner" run over by Lal, whoever that is? Was it Loretta Gibson, taking out the competition? Or Grace, the young girl? Was it someone else entirely who may or may not have a dangerous obsession with me? Or was it an accident? Maybe the driver just got scared and fled the scene. Totally and utterly gutted, I have such a glut of feelings. Deep sadness for this poor woman, along with an illogical responsibility for her even being in this town. My God, is there an adjective that describes heavier than heavy? I leave the store in a daze, hoping against hope that Mrs. Spiner, like *Laura,* isn't really dead. That it was a mistaken identity and that she'll come back and rent some more movies tomorrow.

As I drive home, the urge to stop and vomit in the bougainvillea again grips me, but I take deep breaths and manage to overcome it. I need to see Candy Lou or Cindy Lou or whichever one she is. I need her to hold me and tell me that it wasn't my fault. As she opens the door, I fall into her arms, my body trembling uncontrollably.

She presses me close to her and holds me tight. "What's the matter, baby?" she whispers into my ear.

"Mrs. Spiner was killed. Hit by a car. I feel like I'm to blame. She moved here just to be near me. If she'd just stayed home, she'd still be alive."

From the way she strokes my back, I can tell that she understands my pain. Then . . .

"Well, we can scratch her off the list," she says insensitively.

"That's awfully cold, isn't it?" I ask, surprised by her callousness.

"Look, it's sad, I get it. But I'm more concerned about you. And if there's one less threat out there, so be it. Like I said before, it's our job to protect you."

"Our job?" I ask, hoping to draw her out.

"Yes. My sister's and mine!" she shoots back.

I need to know. I'm starting to feel like I'm James Stewart in Hitchcock's *Vertigo*. And Candy and Cindy are both Kim Novak. Are they the same person? One a blonde, the other brunette?

"Let's cut the bullshit, huh? I can't take it anymore. Are you and Cindy the same person?"

She pulls away from me, a look of anger crossing her face. "You must be kidding," she says, looking at me like I'm a pariah. "Did you sleep with my sister?"

"No, of course not!" I object. "Unless you *are* your sister. Oh, Jesus Christ, I'm just so paranoid about everything right now, I don't know what to think. I mean, you look alike, you talk alike—"

"Okay, cut the Patty Duke shit. You want to know if we're the same person? Call her. Right now."

"Really?" I whimper.

"Yes! Call her!"

As Candy glowers at me, I take Cindy Lou's tattered business card out of my pocket and dial the number.

"Federal Bureau of Investigation. How may I direct your call?"

"Agent Cindy Lou Jones, please."

"One moment," the operator says. "Let me connect you."

With each ring on the extension, my heartbeat quickens. One ring . . . two . . . three . . . Candy Lou and I lock eyes. This is excruciating. Four . . . five . . . six . . . The operator comes back on the line.

"I'm sorry, she's not picking up. Can I take a message? Oh, wait a minute, she just came through the door. Hold on."

For what seems like eternity, everything stops. Until she picks up. "Cindy Lou Jones speaking."

"Hi," I squeak, as if I've never said that word before.

I look over to Candy to gauge how much she detests me in this moment, but she's gone. I want to look for her, talk to her. But . . .

"That was pretty weird today with Reagan, wasn't it?" asks Cindy Lou.

"Yeah." I exhale. "Though for me, the meaning of the word *weird* has reached another level entirely."

"What's up?" she asks.

Nervously shoving my hand into my jacket pocket, I touch

a piece of paper and withdraw it. "Oh, yeah, Genie Francis got another letter from Lal."

I read the letter aloud to her.

"Was the condom included with the letter?"

"Uh, yeah, apparently, but Jonathan didn't give it to me."

"See if he still has it and get it to me if you can. We'll run a DNA test on it."

A pause on the other end.

"Cindy? Oh . . . do you have any new information to tell me?"

"Very good. You're getting the hang of this. Yes, I ran a check on Loretta and Andrew Gibson. Eight months ago they lived in North Carolina. Social Services got a tip from one of the neighbors that she was abusing her child. She denied it. Said the neighbors were confused. They thought they heard her child crying all the time, but that it was actually her. Ultimately, there was no evidence and no charges were filed. Next thing you know, they move to Canada. Makes you wonder."

"Did you find anything on the husband?"

"Nothing. He came up clean. I'm going to check out this Mrs. Spiner person in the morning."

"Oh, that's no longer necessary. I found out at the video store that she was hit by a car and killed."

Another rush of sadness flows through me as I fill her in on Mrs. Spiner's untimely fate.

"What? Gosh, that's a shame," she says sympathetically.

Finally, I'm seeing a difference between these two sisters. One is clearly less jaded and has a bigger heart.

"Well, we can scratch her off the list," she says, bursting

my bubble. "Hey, why don't I drop by and pick up that letter from Lal?"

"Uh, that's probably not a good idea right now. It's kinda late and . . ."

"Is Candy there?" she says, fishing.

"Yeah," I answer reluctantly. "She's been here all day. She wanted to stay in case someone figured out where I lived and—"

"Uh-huh," she cuts me off. "Well, don't do anything you wouldn't do with me. Talk soon."

She hangs up and leaves me a conflicted mess. Now that I know for sure that there are two of them, I'm not certain which one I actually prefer. Obviously, my relationship with Candy has become more intimate. But there's something really intriguing about Cindy. There's a steadiness in her, an inner confidence that's enormously appealing to me, particularly right now. Maybe if we spent more time together, just her and me. And I've always been a sucker for blondes. Not that Candy isn't just as fascinating. She's a wild card. You never know what she's going to do. She's impulsive and unpredictable. And boy, can that girl dance!

"Candy!" I call out. "Where are you?"

Nothing. Maybe she left. I wouldn't blame her. I'm such a putz. I walk through the house, hoping to find her, to explain, to make things right between us. Only one room left. Hoping against hope, I move down the long hallway that leads into the master bedroom. And there I find her lying in my bed, the top sheet only partially concealing her naked body. My favorite outfit of hers. Things are suddenly tilting in her favor.

"Are you mad at me?" I ask, knowing the answer.

"Yes," she answers.

"I had a feeling. I'm really sorry, Candy, and I completely understand your anger. It's just that you and your sister are so alike, and I'm completely out of my mind right now. I'm ridiculous, I know. My paranoia made me think that the two of you might be the same—"

"Shut up," she says, cutting me off.

I feel ashamed and at the same time pleased that I was able to come clean with her. Not so clean that I'm going to tell her that I'm also interested in her sister. I mean, that would require an adult. I'll deal with that later. When the time is right.

"Is there any way I can make it up to you?"

Though she gives me a mysterious smile, I'm pretty certain I decipher its meaning correctly. I free myself of everything except my Calvin Klein briefs and climb under the sheets next to her. As I tuck a lock of her chestnut hair behind her ear and lean in to kiss her neck, my hand slides under her pillow and touches something cold and metallic.

"Is . . . is that your gun under the pillow?" I ask warily.

"Of course," she replies casually.

"Why is your gun in bed with us?"

"I always have my gun close to me. It was there last time. You just didn't know it."

"Listen, if you want me to be honest with you, I have to tell you, I don't love sleeping with a gun in bed with us. It makes me very, very uncomfortable."

"The gun stays," she says bluntly.

I consider her words carefully. It's time to show her who wears the pants in this relationship.

"Okay, no problem."

We do our best to engage in another night of tender terpsichore, but this time it's different. With so much chaos distracting me, I know my performance simply isn't up to par, and we both know it. In fact, it's more of a double bogey. She is kind enough to pretend otherwise. Sometimes the truth is better left unspoken. Uncharacteristically, she falls asleep first. Bored to death, I assume. I toss and turn all night. Thirty minutes of sleep, then an hour awake, ten minutes asleep, then three hours awake. My mind ricocheting from one thought to the next. Lal, Mrs. Spiner, Grace, Candy and Cindy, and Loretta and her child. I half dream a memory of my stepfather.

I'm ten years old. My stepfather, Sol, is saying something to me, but I can't hear him. Each time he speaks, his face grows redder. Whatever it is, he's saying it over and over. Each time he speaks, his face becomes a deeper red. I know that he's about to punish me for some minor infraction. I don't remember what it is. Maybe I forgot to take out the garbage? Or left my shoes under the bed instead of putting them in the closet. That always sent him into a rage. I look at him, and now I can make out what he's saying.

"Which one do you want, son? Belt or board?"

I see that in one hand he holds a leather belt. In the other, a wooden paddle.

I try to lighten the mood, hoping to distract him. "I hate making decisions. I just don't know, I love them both so much!"

That infuriates him and he chooses the belt, all on his own, and

gives me ten whacks across the backside. But I don't cry. And that
makes him even angrier.

"Do you think you've learned your lesson?"

"Hmmm, I can't be sure. Maybe ten more will do the trick."

Furious, he gives me ten more. I still don't cry.

I didn't cry for years after that night.

No breakfast in bed this morning. Sensing Candy is still unhappy with me, I do my best to smooth things over.

"Sorry about last night. I know it wasn't particularly satisfying, but it was nothing to do with you. I had so much on my mind—"

"Yeah, like my sister?" she shoots back.

"What! No! Why in the world would you say that?" I'm not getting any better at this lying thing.

"I'm going home," she says, glaring at me. "These clothes are starting to stand up on their own. Besides, I need to think."

I really don't want her to think. I don't want her to leave, but I can't blame her. Making one last attempt to change her mind, I appeal to the bodyguard in her. "What if something happens while you're gone? What if Lal—"

"Just play it safe. If anything happens, I'm a phone call away. Or call Cindy Lou," she says, throwing one last dart before walking out the door.

We both know things are changing, but I just don't have the courage to deal with it right now.

I'm exhausted, but I manage to drive myself to the studio. In my fatigued state, the workday is grueling, but thankfully brief. As I begin the arduous task of removing my makeup, someone knocks on the trailer door. Throwing on my worn terry-cloth robe, I open the door to find a stranger wearing the familiar mail-boy outfit and carrying a bucket filled with letters.

"Hey, Mr. Spiner, my name's Jimbo. I'm Mickey's replacement."

"What happened to Mickey?" I ask.

"He quit to become a talent manager. He's doing pretty good, too. Got a client a gig writing on *Matlock*. Guy used to be a detective, so I guess he's got a lot of inside knowledge about crime and such."

"Thanks, Jimbo," I say, lifting the bucket inside and closing the door.

Smiling with amusement at the prospect of Tony Orlando and Andy Griffith acting together in a reworking of Ortiz's script originally meant for me, I'm also pleased to find the amount of my fan mail has increased. Rustling through the bucket, I'm relieved to find there is nothing new from Lal. However, one letter jumps out at me. Postmarked from Canada.

Dear Brent,

Thank you so much for the call last night. It did so much to brighten my spirits. Andrew has been very cold to me since he discovered the letters I've written to you. He told me he threatened you. I'm so sorry for that. Please don't worry, Brent. I won't let anything happen to you.

I suppose I shouldn't have made copies of them, but I wanted to remember exactly what I said. Reading them over and over makes me feel closer to you.

I've made a big decision. I'm going to leave Andrew. I would come to you if you want me. All you have to do is say the word and I'll jump on the next plane. I could leave my daughter with Andrew, and after we've had some time alone, wink wink, I could send for her. Just say the word.

Oh, and you should know that if I come, I will need a firm mattress. I've had back problems for years.

Please call me tonight. I long to hear your voice. I long for many things. But we can talk about that later.

With love (not luv),
Loretta Gibson

I put Loretta's letter in my jacket to save it for Cindy Lou. I had pretty much ruled Loretta out as a suspect, but I just don't know. Finishing the removal of my makeup, I find that the Eliminate has almost eliminated the top layer of my skin, so I decide to visit the only person I know who can remedy my damaged derma. Marla the Marvelous Facialist.

TWENTY-ONE   FACE OFF

THE STUDIO OF Marla the Marvelous Facialist is just a few blocks away. She calls it a studio, and rightfully so, because she really is an artist. Paramount generously pays for me to have facials every now and then, because of potential embarrassment. In the future, androids don't have zits. Marla is one of a kind. She takes great care to make sure her clients get not only her professional best, but her personal best. Marla operates as sort of a therapist for me and everyone else she serves. I lie down on a comfortable bed, she flips on the Vivaldi, and the show begins. After gently squeezing every pore on my punim, she places pads on both cheeks. These pads are attached to electrodes running back to a central machine, which she can dial from 1 to 10 in intensity. When she gets to around 3 or 4, I sense a metallic taste in my mouth and a slightly uncomfortable stinging in my face. One can only imagine what 10 feels like, so I'm always on my best behavior.

"Are you comfy?" she asks. "Do you want a blanket?"

"No, thanks, Marla. This is perfect."

"Deanna was here yesterday."

She jokingly calls Marina Sirtis by her character name, Deanna Troi. She also seems to think Marina has magical empathetic qualities in real life. Which she actually does. She probably refers to me as Data when I'm not there.

"You look terrible. Your skin looks like shit. Red, raw shit. Are you getting *any* sleep?"

Marla's not one for mincing words. I appreciate that about her.

"No, I'm having the worst insomnia. I slept, like, a total of about an hour last night."

"You want to talk about it?" she asks with genuine sympathy.

Since I've booked only an hour session, I give her the *Reader's Digest* version of the nightmare I've been living through. I tell her about Lal and Loretta and Mrs. Spiner and Grace, and even about Cindy Lou and Candy Lou. The look she gives me, I've seen on my mother's face. Sort of a combination of sadness and a need to help. However, what she does next my mother would never dream of. Marla opens a cabinet below her workstation and removes a large clear plastic bag full of pills. And when I say *large,* I mean like trash bag size. She opens it, fishes out one pill, drops it into my palm, then hands me a plastic cup of water to wash it down.

"What is it?" I ask.

"A Quaalude. It'll help you relax. You take a nap. We'll talk more when you wake up."

Wow. A Quaalude! I haven't seen Quaaludes in years. And

it's probably been ten or twelve years since I've taken one. I had just moved to Hollywood and was living in an apartment near San Vicente. A friend and I were going to breakfast one morning, and when he arrived to pick me up, he had a couple of Mexican Quaaludes with him. No idea why they were from Mexico, but that's what he said. I had a very important meeting with a major casting director scheduled for later in the afternoon. I rationalized that if I took it immediately, I'd be fine by midday. We swallowed the pills and went to Canter's Deli on Fairfax, where I ordered my usual, a smoked salmon platter with a sesame seed bagel. The next thing I remember, I was sitting on the floor of my apartment watching a rerun of *All in the Family* at three in the afternoon. Everything between the smoked salmon and Archie Bunker was completely erased, and I had just twenty minutes to make it to my very important meeting at 20th Century Fox. Somehow I drove there and managed to charm the major casting director. By the time I got home, I had no idea what we talked about. Later, my breakfast companion called to tell me he had taught a class that day at UCLA and had no memory of what he lectured about. He could recall only that one of the students stopped him on his way out of class and told him it was life changing. I hope this Quaalude of Marla's isn't from Mexico. Either way, I'm taking it. I suck down the pill with the water, lie back on the cushioned table, and close my eyes. Soon I feel like everything is . . . slowing down . . . like I'm deep inside a . . . thick rubber tire slowly rolling into a deep dream . . . My heartbeat is in my ears making a peculiar sound . . . THUNK . . . THUNK . . . THUNK . . .

I'm driving a taxicab in New York City again. The young man in the white suit and the bloody ass is still pounding the butt of his knife into the ceiling like a madman. THUNK . . . THUNK . . . THUNK . . .

"*GO! GO!*" *he shrieks.*

"*Okay, just please don't hurt me!*" *I beg.*

I drive in a panic, looking around for any sign that points the way to a hospital. I can't even tell where we are. I can't think. I'm too frightened to think! I see another man in a white suit walking on the sidewalk, so I pull over to ask him directions. But before I speak, the man in the back seat yells out again.

"*THAT'S MY BROTHER!!!!*"

"*What?*" *I gasp.* "*How crazy is that? I was just about to ask this random guy for directions, and he turns out to be—*"

"*SHUT UP!*" *he screams, sending a spray of spittle onto the glass partition of the taxi.*

The brother opens the door, jumps in the back seat, and yells at me. "*41 SIMPSON STREET! SOUTH BRONX!!!! GO!!!!*"

I really don't want to go there. One of my coworkers was pulled out of his cab and beaten into a coma in that neighborhood. So I begin babbling nonsensically.

"*That's Fort Apache, isn't it? You, know, when the movie* Fort Apache, the Bronx *came out, I stupidly thought it was a remake of the John Wayne and Henry Fonda picture. But then it turned out to be a Paul Newman and Ed Asner movie. Did you guys think the same—*"

"SHUT UP AND DRIVE!" the brothers shouted in tandem.

"Okay! But I have no idea how to get there! Please! Maybe another cab will know the way," I plead.

The brother begins calling out turn-by-turn directions. I hit the accelerator and speed down the empty streets. I think we're going to a hospital, but it turns out to be an apartment building. The first brother, the one with the stabbed ass, yells at me.

"WE'RE GOING TO GET SOME CASH FOR YOU IN-SIDE!!! WE'LL BE RIGHT BACK!!!"

The two brothers jump out of the cab and run inside the building. I turn around and look at the blood on the back seat. I try to mop it up with my jacket, but it just smears into the cracked leather upholstery. Then I wait. And wait. Looking at the broken windows in the buildings and the blown-out streetlamps, I sit there in the dark, thinking, This is crazy. What am I doing here? Then it occurs to me that maybe the guy wasn't stabbed in his ass by his girlfriend at all. Maybe that isn't really blood. There's probably not even a girlfriend. This is a setup. Someone is probably going to jump in my cab and kill me!

I throw the gearshift into drive and just as I'm about to stomp on the accelerator, I see someone in the rearview mirror running on the sidewalk toward the building. It's a young woman wearing a T-shirt with blood on it. She's holding a large bloody knife in her hand and has a determined, angry look on her face. I watch her as she runs up to the call box and presses a button. A yelling voice comes over the speaker. It sounds like one of the brothers.

"WHAT DO YOU WANT???"

"LET ME IN OR I'M GONNA STAB HIM IN HIS ASS AGAIN!"

There's a pause and then the door buzzes. The young woman in the bloody T-shirt with the bloody knife opens the door and runs into the building. I imagine they're inside now, making up.

I'm not sure how that works when you have knife wounds in your ass, but there's nothing more exciting than making up after a bad fight. I'm sure no one is coming back to pay me. Although they might be inside planning how to kill me! I drive away like a bat out of hell.

When I open my eyes, Marla is leaning over me, smiling. I'm woozy from the Quaalude.

"You were having a bad dream, weren't you?"

"Ah, yeah, how did you know?"

"You said, 'Someone's going to kill me.' Strange. Those pills are supposed to relax you."

"I was dreaming about something that actually happened to me. I was driving a cab and a woman stabbed a man in his ass and then she threatened to do it again."

"Obviously this nightmare of yours has even permeated your unconscious mind. I took the liberty while you were sleeping to consult the *I Ching*. I asked for knowledge that would help you conquer the fear that is overwhelming you. This is what I found."

She opens a book of translations from the *I Ching*. She reads it aloud:

"'Waiting in the meadow, it furthers one to abide in what endures.

"'The danger is not yet close. One is still waiting in the open plain. There is a feeling of something impending. Something dangerous. One must continue to lead a regular life as long as possible. Only in this way does one guard against a premature waste of strength.'"

I think that Marla must be some kind of shaman, even though I have no clue what the hell she's talking about. Maybe I'd understand if I wasn't so stoned.

"What does that mean, Marla?"

"It means you've got to knock it off. You're so afraid this person is going to kill you that you've already stopped living. For all you know, it's just some kook having fun scaring a C-list celebrity."

"Oh, come on, I'm at least a B minus, aren't I?"

"Whatever. The point is, as long as you're alive, live! If, indeed, someone tries to hurt you, at least you can face that moment without fear. Definitely improves your chances."

I consider the logic of what Marla has told me with what's left of my brain.

"This has been going on for a while now. Has anyone actually come to harm?" she asks.

"Well, a postal worker cut his finger."

"See what I mean?" she says.

She's right. Nothing really terrible has happened. Just a few bloody letters and a pig's penis. Maybe Lal is just trying to scare me. No one's died. And then I remember Mrs. Spiner. Tonight is the celebration of the life of Mrs. Spiner. I was feeling too frightened to go by myself, but now dammit, I want to go! Well, I don't really want to go, but I feel I owe it to her or at least to myself. Guilt, like fear, is another thing I have to learn to let go of.

I thank her for the facial and the wisdom and the Quaalude and walk out into a blindingly bright sunset. I poke around in my pockets, find my sunglasses, and give my peepers a rest. A T-shirt and jeans seems inappropriate for a somber occasion, so I drive home, as best I can, to put on something more presentable. When I get to my house, I decide to grab my mail before heading inside. Nothing much. A flyer for 10 percent off at Zankou Chicken, a bill from California Edison, and . . . a letter from Lal.

Typically, it is smeared with blood.

> *Dear Daddy,*
>
> *I'll bet you have a really nice house. I could've been happy living there with you. But you let me die. And now I want you to be with me. Where I am. I've come from such a long way away. But now I'm so close. And I'm excited to finally be united with you. Family is everything. Isn't it?*
>
> *Your loving daughter,*
> *Lal*

Oh my God! She knows where I live! I need to call Cindy Lou and tell her about this. But, if I call her now, I'll be late to Mrs. Spiner's shindig. I'll call her in the morning. I'm feeling oddly calm. Must be Marla's lessons? Or maybe the Quaalude? Either way, it feels good. I go inside and waste about fifteen minutes just admiring my clothes. I grab a jacket, toss it over my T-shirt, and hurry off to pay my respects.

TWENTY-TWO   FRIENDS AND STRANGERS

I REMEMBER THAT Jeff said the event was at a church on Gower, but what was it? I cruise down Gower scanning for it. *First* something or other. Episcopal, maybe? I know it's gotta be close. Oncoming car headlights are blurry. I really shouldn't be driving in this condition. I'm about to turn back when I see a church with a sign in front: FIRST PRESBYTERIAN CHURCH OF HOLLYWOOD. Yes, that's it! A redbrick building with arched doorways below a beautiful bell tower that stretches up into the night sky, a lit cross atop reaching for the stars.

Heading inside, I find a group of about ten people sitting in chairs facing a podium, behind which is a simple white coffin. Lying in the coffin is a deceased woman, maybe in her early thirties, with a pleasant look on her face. I move closer to the coffin and look inside. Mrs. Spiner doesn't really resemble Jodie Foster at all. More like Helen Hunt. Though I guess you could say they sort of resemble each other. Mostly she just looks like herself, whoever that is. I look around at the mourners, who are all staring at me. I approach a middle-aged woman, trying not to slur my words, trying to keep it together.

"Excuse me, did you know her?"

"Yes. We were in acting class together," says the woman.

"What is her name?" I inquire as gently as possible.

"Uh, well, she called herself Mrs. Spiner."

"Right, I know that, but do you know her real name?"

"No, she never told us."

I turn to a group of three people sitting nearby. "Excuse me, do you know what her real name is?"

All three people speak more or less simultaneously. "Mrs. Spiner," they say.

"Oh, for fuck's sake!" I say to myself a little too audibly.

Everyone in the room hears me. They're all silent. I gesture toward the deceased, just a few feet away from me. I can see they're starting to put together who I am.

"Didn't anyone know this woman? Didn't any of you actually *know* her?" I say, increasingly agitated.

One woman in the back pipes up. "I thought she was your wife."

"She liked to talk about *you*," says a tiny voice in the front row.

A very delicate-looking young woman is obviously talking about me.

"She moved to Los Angeles to be closer to you. She told us that all the time. Besides acting, her favorite activity was to talk about you."

"PEOPLE, THIS IS NOT ABOUT ME!" I yell. "THIS IS ABOUT HER!"

There is an awkward silence as everyone continues staring at me. Feeling bony fingers touching my elbow, I turn to see an old priest standing beside me.

"I know this must be difficult for you in your hour of grief, but as the bereaved husband, would you like to say a few words, Mr. Spiner?"

"Father, I'm not . . ."

"It's Reverend," he corrects me, "Presbyterians aren't priests."

"Oh, sorry. Reverend. Look, I'm not her husband. I've never met her," I say, trying to stay civil.

He gazes soulfully into my eyes, a beatific smile on his lips. "Nonetheless, I'm sure she would appreciate you offering a few kind words. As would the rest of the congregation. You know, they all chipped in to purchase that lovely spray of flowers."

He points to a crummy bowl of flowers, already turning brown, in front of the casket.

"They're gladiolas," he enlightens me. "They represent strength and character in life. By the way, my sermon last Sunday was about that very thing. And ironically, I spoke about Data, and in particular, the episode 'The Offspring.' How you showed such strength and character in the way you accepted the loss of your daughter, Lal."

"Oh . . . my . . . God," I whisper to myself in disbelief.

The thought of speaking sends shivers up my spine, but I guess I can ad-lib as well as anyone in the room, so what the fuck? I mean, she was a fan of mine. Maybe she was deluded, but she still deserves respect. She deserves acknowledgment. I walk to the pulpit, look at the mourners, all ten of them, and clear my throat. The effect of the Quaalude is still clouding my mind, but I press on.

"I didn't know Mrs. Spiner . . . very well. In fact, I've never even seen her until now," I say looking back to the casket. "But I feel . . . somewhat . . . somehow . . . responsible . . . for her death. I didn't hit her with that car, but I can't help but feel that she would still be alive if it weren't for me. She saw me on her TV and I became a friend to her. Dr. Oliver Sacks, do you know who he is? Well, he said that to me about many of his patients. They see me as a friend. So of course, like all friends do, she wanted to be near me. But all her feelings for me were the result of an illusion. I wasn't her friend. I didn't know her. And all the qualities she loved about me . . . they're not real. They are the qualities of a fictional character who is actually very, very different from me. This is a mirage called acting. Surrounded by another mirage called celebrity."

The young woman speaks again.

"I thought this wasn't about you?" she challenges.

"It's not about me. It's about her," I say.

"Well, you're still making it all about you," she counters.

"Because I didn't *know* her! How can I talk about her? I don't know anything about her! And neither do any of you!"

The young woman stands defiantly and raises her voice.

"But we know that she related to something in us! And we related to something in her. And you know that she related to good things inside you! Those things that you brought to your character, whether you want to admit that or not. You know that parts of you resonated with parts of her! So we all actually know a lot about her, because we know a lot about ourselves! And those parts of her that we share, those emotions, they are real! No matter what you think!"

I'm stunned into silence. I'm not sure I completely understand what she is saying, but there's something genuine and loving about it. I'm about to tell her that when a man with a beard stands and raises his hand.

"Mr. Spiner, not to change the subject, but when you beam out, is that an effect, or are your molecules really dispersing?" asks the bearded man.

Once again, I'm stunned into total silence. Finally I'm able to speak. Sort of. "Uh, no, that's, that's an effect."

I turn away, hoping to avoid any more insensitive questions, and look at Mrs. Spiner in her coffin. Her eyes are closed and a teeny smile is on her face, its true meaning hidden to me. I hope she was having pleasant thoughts as she transitioned from this world.

"Rest in peace, Mrs. Spiner," I say to her. "I have to go now."

When I turn back to the congregation, five of the mourners have lined up by the front door. As I move toward them, they each hold out pieces of paper. These are clumsily printed flyers with Mrs. Spiner's picture on the front. Or is that Helen Hunt? One of the mourners hands me a Sharpie.

"Could you sign it underneath her picture, Mr. Spiner?"

I like to think that if I hadn't been so wasted, I'd have refused.

And I'd tell them they should be ashamed of themselves. But as I want to get the hell out of there, I shame myself and sign them all. Hoping to say a polite goodbye, I turn to the minister, who appeared to be scrounging for something behind one of the pews. He pulled out a Bible, ripped a page out of the front, and handed it to me for my signature. From Exodus, I presume.

✳

I'm glad to be back in my car. There's always something about shooting through the world in the safety of my own private bubble that makes me happy. The effects of the Quaalude have yet to wear off, and I'm growing desperate for sleep. My driving is becoming even more erratic than it was earlier. I think I just ran a red light, but I can't be sure. I'm starting to hear a disturbing hum in my ears that keeps growing louder and louder. Wait, that's not a hum—that's a siren, and according to my rearview mirror, it seems to be coming from a car with a flashing red light attached to it. Oh shit, I'm going to get busted! This is really bad. I could get fired for this. Like most actors, I don't read my contracts, but there's probably something in there about not driving on Quaaludes. Slowly pulling to the curb, I take extra care not to drive over it. A uniformed cop who if he had been wearing a Hawaiian shirt would look shockingly like Tom Selleck gets out of his car and walks to the driver's side window. I smile up at him. He doesn't smile at me. He just does circles with his index finger, universal mime for "roll down the window." Okay, now he definitely knows I'm stoned. I roll down the window.

"Sorry, Officer, I keep my windows so clean, I thought it was already down."

"You ran that red light on Fountain. You in a hurry?" he says in that no-nonsense police sort of way.

"No, sir, but you see, I have this visual abnormality, and sometimes I have a hard time distinguishing between red and green. It's a medical condition."

"May I see your driver's license, please?"

"Yes, sir."

My hands shaking, I slide my license out of my wallet and hand it to him. He studies it a little too meticulously, then looks at me. I know what he's thinking. I had a moustache when the picture was taken, and I weighed about twenty pounds less. No way he believes it's me. I'm going to jail.

"Step out of the car, Mr. Mintz," he says.

My license identifies me as Brent Spiner Mintz. Mintz was Sol's last name. That was my name from the time I was six. After Sol married my mother, he legally adopted my brother and me and changed our names from Spiner to Mintz. We were okay with that. We liked him. For about a week. And then he changed.

"Do you think you can walk a straight line, Mr. Mintz?"

When I was thirteen, my mother had had enough, and so had we. He got visitation rights in the divorce, so my brother and I had to go to the movies with him every other Sunday for about a year. Then he stopped coming. The last time I saw him, he asked me to talk to my mother and tell her to take him back. I said, "No, you're not well. You need help." I was fourteen. He died a couple of years later of a brain aneurysm, like my friend Trey did. It was speculated that the pressure in his brain might have accounted for his anger and violence.

"Mr. Mintz, can you hear me?"

When I became an actor, I changed my name professionally to Spiner. It was like an enormous weight lifted from my soul when I rid myself of his name. I wish I could get rid of all of him.

"Mr. Mintz, I'm going to have to ask you to put your hands on the car," says the officer.

"See, that's my legal name." I say, turning around and following his orders. "But I'm just not used to anyone calling me that anymore. My middle name on my license is what I go by. Spiner. Brent Spiner."

The policeman slowly walks to my side so he can get a good look at me. The dumbest look washes over his face. He grabs the sides of his head in utter disbelief. "DATA? HOLY SHIT! YOU'RE DATA!"

"Yes," I am not at all sorry to say in this moment, "yes, I am Data. Do you watch the show?"

"Watch it? I'm obsessed with it! And fuck me, you're my favorite character! DATA!"

He embraces me, literally lifting me off the ground. After I sign the back of his ticket book, he gives me a very gentle warning, shakes my hand vigorously, and before parting, gives me one of those "friend of the police" cards to get me off the next time I break a traffic law. Sometimes being on this show is a blessing. Actually, lots of times. I learned a couple of very important lessons tonight. Never do drugs and drive. And if you ever change your name like I did, like Mrs. Spiner did, make sure you let people know who you really are.

When I get home, the house feels different. Candy isn't here. And even though the letter from Lal that I found in my mailbox is still deeply concerning, I manage to immerse myself in the mystical meditations of Marla and relax into a rare restful night's sleep.

TWENTY-THREE THE GREAT BIRD

AROUND NOON THE next day, I'm at work in a scene with Patrick and Gates on the Sickbay set when a call comes from the producers for us to immediately stop what we're doing and report to the Bridge. I assume, since it has happened before, that we're in for a reprimand about our rowdy behavior. We are a raucous cast. We have to be. When you work sixteen hours a day on sound stages with no windows, either you laugh a lot or you go mad. We chose laughter. Our last lecture from the producers came when a very good director refused to come back because he found the cast "out of control." Fully expecting the worst, I find my understanding of those words changes dramatically when the entire company, every department, pours through the doors of Stage 9. It's instantly clear that something terrible has happened. Rick Berman, our executive producer, asks for our attention, and calmly delivers the very difficult news that Gene Roddenberry, the Great Bird of the Galaxy, had passed away that morning. To those of us who have been around him recently, this doesn't come as a huge surprise. He had been in ill health, and his years of living life to the fullest had taken their toll. Each of us embraces the news of his death in our own way, tears from some, others merely stunned into respectful silence. One hairdresser screams, "Noooo!!!" and falls to her knees sobbing, despite having never met Gene. A memorial service is planned for Sunday and we are all invited to attend. We are instructed to take a short break and then to resume the day's work because "that's the way Gene would've wanted it." Though how they know that, I have no idea.

On Sunday afternoon, I don an appropriate suit and drive alone to Forest Lawn Memorial Park in the Hollywood Hills. I wander around the gigantic green property before the service is scheduled to begin. Something about this place eases the fear that has gripped most waking hours of my recent life. Maybe it's the reality that if Lal were to kill me where I stand, at least a lot of travel wouldn't be necessary. It is already a moving experience to be walking among the burial sites of so many of my heroes, particularly Buster Keaton and Stan Laurel. I stop in front of Stan's and Buster's grave sites for at least twenty minutes each, just smiling, my way of thanking them for all the joy they've given me. I stroll around a bit more, paying my respects to the various stars who've taken up residence in these hallowed grounds, when I am approached by a couple of young guys. One is wearing a gold Star Trek uniform from the original series, and the other is dressed in a dark suit that doesn't exactly fit but is nonetheless fitting for the occasion. Their demeanor is deadly serious, and I fight to stifle a laugh when I see that the guy in the suit also wears a pair of pointed Vulcan ears.

"Mr. Spiner?" the Vulcan says, "forgive our intrusion, but we wanted to offer our condolences on the passing of Mr. Roddenberry. He meant so much to us."

"To all of us," I reply.

Reaching into a bag, the Starfleet officer withdraws a stack of papers with some sort of drawing on them and hands one to me. "We made these for you and the rest of the cast," he says, "and for anyone else who wants one. We call it 'The Three Giants of Science Fiction.'"

I look closely at the picture, which consists of three clumsily drawn figures: Shakespeare, Gene, and . . .

"That's Alexander Graham Bell, isn't it?" I ask, confused.

"Oh no, sir, that's Jules Verne."

"Oh. Of course. Well, they did look a lot alike," I say, trying to save the moment. "But Shakespeare?

"We like to think of Shakespeare as the first great sci-fi writer. You know, the classic film *Forbidden Planet* was based on his play *The Tempest*?"

"Absolutely true, and was there ever a better Prospero than Walter Pidgeon? I wonder if he's buried here," I say, trying to disengage. "Maybe I'll have a look around."

"Thank you for your time, sir," says Spock in a suit. "If it's any comfort to you, we pledge to preserve Gene's vision for as long as we live."

They both hold up one hand making Spock's renowned symbol signifying *Live Long and Prosper.*

As they back away, I awkwardly return the sign, though in truth, my fingers don't ever get that exactly right. But they deserve the attempt. Feeling guilty at my initial impulse to laugh, I appreciate their dedication to something bigger than them, and certainly bigger than me.

When it is time to begin the memorial, I enter the Hall of Liberty and sit with my castmates from the show. Unlike Mrs. Spiner's evening of remembrance, this event is packed. Friends, coworkers, and family occupy the main floor of what seems like a huge theater, while a few hundred fans watch from the balcony. The ceremony begins with a film of photos and reminiscences of Gene from his boyhood to his last days, including many shots of him at work and at leisure. Nichelle Nichols, Uhura from the original *Star Trek,* sings a couple of numbers, including one that she wrote, appropriately titled "Gene." The speakers range from close compatriots to fellow writers to TV and movie stars. Whoopi Goldberg speaks about her experience of watching *Star Trek* from the projects and how it gave her hope to see a black woman making a contribution in the future. Patrick, as usual, is eloquent in reminding the congregation of a beautiful scene that Gene had written about the ambiguity of death. But for me, the high point of the service is the great writer Ray Bradbury. He rhapsodizes about *Star Trek* and how it "stands out in a sea of violence, as a nice, quiet, moral example of fine entertainment at a time when we need it." He talks about how he has often been mistaken for Gene and that he'd always responded by saying, "Thank you, I'm glad you like my work." But it's his last line that really moves me. He says he'd been mistaken for Gene at the airport just the day before. A young fellow had come up to him and said, "Mr. Roddenberry, I heard you died?" And he answered the kid, "No. No, I'm still alive." And so he is. And always will be.

After the service, we adjourn to a large patio outside, all of us grouped together, family, friends, and fans. There are news crews and paparazzi circling, waiting for something to sell, but mostly everyone ignores them. It strikes me, looking at the faces of his devotees, many dressed in Starfleet uniforms, that these are like his progeny, mourning the passing of their spiritual father. Their loss is as real, as great, as anyone's there. It's heartwarming and satisfying to be a part of something united by hope and a better future. A squadron of four Air Force jets flies overhead, the salute to the missing man. And on this crisp November day, we all look to the sky and beyond.

TWENTY-FOUR THE SWITCHEROO

SLEEPING IN IS something I haven't done much of lately, but fortunately my name doesn't appear on today's call sheet. It's heaven to luxuriate between the covers, not concerned about anything other than on which side to sleep. When I was a young actor living in New York, sharing a railroad apartment with two friends, I had a sign on my bedroom door that read: "To be with one's self in peaceful slumber is perhaps the greatest gift of all." That's how serious I am about sleep. Glorious, peaceful sleep.

Ding-dong, interrupts the bell at my front door. *Ding-dong.*

Shit, who the hell is this? Sliding out of my dreamspace and into my Uggs, I take a few steps toward . . . Wait, what if it's Lal, just waiting for me to open the door? But why would she ring the bell? Who would think of ringing the bell and then killing someone when they answer it? *Hmm.* Of course she's funny like that. I wish Candy was here, or at least her gun was. I grab my trusty baseball bat and barely crack the shutters on the bedroom window. Craning my neck, I can almost see the front door. All I can make out is an arm. It appears to be a uniform of some sort with a patch on the sleeve. Fetching my glasses from the nightstand, I take an optically enhanced look. USPS. Holy shit! What if Lal works for the post office? Of course, that's how she was able to have the letters postmarked from different locations! The figure at the door takes a step back and . . . Oh, for fuck's sake, it's my mailman, Ken.

"Coming!" I shout toward the living room.

Wait a minute, what if Ken is Lal? He never comes to the door. He always uses the mailbox, and if there's a package, he leaves it on the stoop. But why would Ken want to kill me? We get along really well, and I always give him a good tip at Christmas, and that's right around the corner. I'm starting to get edgy and paranoid again. Maybe I should've taken a few Quaaludes for the road.

Throwing caution to the wind, I go to the front door and open it. "Hey, Ken. What's up?"

He stands there sizing me up with his mouth agape. It's only then that I realize I'm wearing nothing but my underwear and a pair of Uggs, while holding a Louisville Slugger in my hand.

"What's the matter, Ken," I continue, "haven't you ever seen a half-naked man with a baseball bat?"

"Only in my dreams, Mr. Spiner, only in my dreams."

"Sorry, I was in bed and I thought . . . oh, never mind, come on in while I grab a robe."

Ken is a very decent guy. He's been my mailman ever since

I moved into this house four years ago. We've had a number of conversations in the past, but always by the mailbox. He's an enormous film buff, and not surprisingly, of sci-fi in particular. I'm sure he's seen more episodes of my show than I have, but he's always been cool about it, asking only penetrating questions and making astute observations. I consider him a friend of sorts, and I'm always glad to see him. He seems to have more on his mind today than discussing the comparative values of the mechanical triad of Data, C-3PO, and Robby the Robot. I can see it in his troubled face.

"Is something wrong, Ken?" I ask.

He pulls two cards from his back pocket. "Well, Mr. Spiner, I, uh, I got these two change-of-address cards. People fill these out when they're moving to another location. Are you moving, Mr. Spiner?"

"No, what?"

He looks intently at the two cards in his hand, trying to make sense of them. "This card was sent to the post office. It says you want all your mail delivered to an address in Kansas City, Kansas."

"Kansas City? I've never even been to Kansas City."

"And this other card was filled out asking for a . . . Dr. Sandra Ogilvy's mail to be sent to this address."

"I really don't understand, Ken," I say, slightly alarmed.

"So you do want your mail to keep coming here?" he asks.

"Yes, of course."

"And you don't want these letters of hers I have here?"

"No! God, no. Send them back," I object.

"Hmm, must be some kind of computer fuckup," he surmises.

I know deep down it's more than that. But I couldn't possibly explain it to him. Or even to myself.

"Well, I'm glad you're not leaving, Mr. Spiner. There aren't many people on my route that I can discuss everything from Kubrick to Cronenberg with. Not many people in my life, for that matter."

Ken turns away and heads for the door. "I guess I'd better get a move on, Mr. Spiner. People don't get much real mail anymore. Just bills and junk mail. But they'll be waiting for their junk," he says, starting off.

"Hey, Ken, come by anytime. We can talk movies. Oh, and don't you think it's about time you called me Brent?"

We high-five and he hightails it to the house next door as I hightail it to the phone to call Agent Cindy Lou Jones.

"FBI, how can I direct your call?"

"Agent Cindy Lou Jones, please."

Please, please, please be there.

"Agent Jones speaking."

"Cindy. Agent Jones, it's Brent. Oh my God, I've got so much to tell you. I got two more letters, one from Lal and one from Loretta. And the strangest thing just happened."

"Save it." She cuts me off. "Are you at home?"

"Uh, yeah."

"I'll be right over," she says and hangs up.

Jeez, this is kind of exciting. She's coming over. I haven't had a woman over at my place since, well, since Candy Lou. Maybe

I should make hors d'oeuvres? There's a nice block of Velveeta in the fridge . . . Nah, that'll look like I'm trying to impress her. But I definitely need to put on some clothes. Around forty-five minutes later, the doorbell rings. After having tried on a variety of looks, I settled on my usual ensemble of T-shirt and jeans. Better to be myself. I open the door and there she stands, brown-suited and beautiful, that ever-engaging no-nonsense look on her face.

"Hi. Come in. You look great," I say, gesturing her in.

I knew as soon as the words came out of my mouth I'd made a mistake. She clearly has no interest in how I think she looks. She ignores the unfortunate comment and drifts into the living room.

"So, what's happened?" she asks, in full professional mode.

"Well, like I said on the phone, I got a couple of new letters. Would you like to sit down?" I offer.

"No thanks. Could I see the letters? You also mentioned that something strange occurred?"

"Yeah, my mailman, Ken, came by. He had two change-of-address cards. Apparently someone asked for my mail to be forwarded to Dr. Ogilvy's address in Kansas City, and for hers to be forwarded here."

"Interesting," she remarks mysteriously.

A pause hangs in the air while we stare at each other, both waiting for the next question.

"Do you want to ask me something?" she finally says, breaking the silence.

"Oh. Right, I have to ask you or you can't tell me."

"Bingo," she replies, a slight smile cracking the corners of her mouth.

"Well, first of all, why is Dr. Ogilvy in Kansas City? Doesn't she work in Duluth?"

"Not anymore, I'm afraid. I called the institute last week to see if she'd heard anything from or about the missing girl. I was informed that she's no longer working there. The institute has an ironclad policy about revealing the case studies of their patients. Doctor-patient privilege, they call it. So when she gave us information about the girl, she breached this policy and was fired for it. We investigated further and found that Dr. Ogilvy has relocated to Kansas City and opened a private practice there. I guess it's our fault, poor woman. She gave us that information only because she thought your life was in danger."

"That's shitty," I say, "she was just trying to help. I feel kind of guilty."

"Yeah, well, rules," she replies. "Everyone has them."

Another pause lingers until I get that she wants me to ask more.

"So why the switcheroo? Why is our mail being directed to each other?"

"It seems our Grace, besides being sick, is a very clever little girl. She's toying with both of you now."

"Wow, that's pretty devious," I say, stating the obvious. "So Grace is Lal?"

"It certainly looks that way."

"I guess that lets Loretta off the hook," I add.

"I would assume so," she answers. "Now we just have to find Grace before—"

"Before she kills me." I gulp.

Cindy looks down at the letters in her hand. A thought wrinkles her brow.

"One other thing. Did you notice there's no stamp on this letter from Lal? She didn't mail it. Not only does she know where you live . . . she's been here."

This new piece of information seems to evaporate all of the blood from my head. My legs turn to jelly and I'm on my way to the floor when Cindy catches me mid-drop. If there's one thing I hate, it's having the vapors in front of a woman, not that that's ever happened to me before.

"Easy there, champ," she says, plopping me into the nearest chair. "I'll get you some water."

She finds her way to the kitchen, returns with a bottle of Arrowhead, and sits next to me on the arm of the chair.

"Here you go," she says as she opens the bottle and guides the water into my dry-as-dust mouth. "That's a good boy."

As I gulp it down, I look up into her eyes. I can see that she's worried, too. And not just like an FBI agent worries. Like someone who cares.

"What am I going to do, Cindy?"

She thinks a moment, then offers: "I can have someone watch the house for a day or two, but if nothing happens, I can't justify it to the agency. After that, call Candy."

"Can't you stay?"

"No, I should go now."

"Okay," I murmur, implying "please don't."

As she rises to leave, I call out to her. "Hey . . . listen, I'm scared and I'm confused. I like Candy, I really do. But I don't know if it's because she reminds me of you or—"

"Stop. This isn't right. And it's not all your fault. I shouldn't have flirted with you. Maybe sibling rivalry got the best of me. But I'm an FBI agent, first and foremost. And getting involved on a case is against regulations. Like I said, rules."

"Just, please, I'm just not sure Candy and I are right for each other. Maybe I was so traumatized that I just reached out to the nearest body, so to speak. I know this is awkward and kind of scummy of me, given that I slept with your sister, but maybe when this is all over and you're not on the case anymore . . . If I'm still alive, can I call you or something?"

She looks at me for a long beat. About the length of a Wagnerian opera.

"When this is over, if you're not still sweet on Candy and you're still alive . . ." With her final thought suspended in the air, she turns and walks out the door.

God, I'm such a putz.

TWENTY-FIVE   A CHRISTMAS CAROL

FOR THE NEXT couple of days, FBI agents sit in a car in front of my house, watching, waiting for someone to kill me. As I peek at them through the shutters, they look like FBI from central casting. If they'd been on my case in the first place, I wouldn't be in this conundrum with the Jones girls, though I'm sure I'd have found some other way to complicate my life. That's the way I roll. On the third day, I look through the shutters again, they've taken their leave, and I'm alone again with my paranoia and my fear. I think about calling Candy to come over, but I'm not ready to face her. What can I say to her? "I'm really fond of you, but I think your identical twin might be a better fit?" This week is a Riker-heavy episode, and since I don't work again until Monday and I have enough food in the house to sustain me, I decide to hole up here, never going out into potential catastrophe. I keep the shutters closed and the lights off in hopes that if Lal, or Grace, comes by she'll think I'm not home. The days crawl by and there is nothing. No Lal, no letters, nothing. Maybe Grace has grown weary of this charade? Maybe she's had her fun and is satisfied leaving me to wonder forever if she'll leap out of the darkness when my guard is down. I've had a lot of time to think about the situation with Cindy and Candy—how I'm going to handle it. Which one do I really want? And do either of them really want me? This is hell. By the end of the week, I'm growing claustrophobic. I need to get out, to be with people, to live in the real world. Tomorrow Patrick is presenting, for the first time, his one-man show of *A Christmas Carol* at Caltech in Pasadena. I had promised to be there, and I really want to go. But the idea of going alone sends shivers through me. Some of my castmates are going, and I could hitch a ride, but I don't want them coming to my house, putting their lives in possible danger.

So I break down and call Candy. "Hey!" I say, as if nothing had happened between us. "How do you feel about Dickens?"

"Who's Dickens?"

"Charles Dickens, of course. Patrick is doing his one-man show of *A Christmas Carol* tomorrow and I was thinking maybe you'd like to—"

"Be your bodyguard?" she says. Interesting how both Jones girls have a habit of finishing my sentences.

"Uh, yeah. Things have kind of ramped up with the Lal situation lately, and I don't really—"

"Feel safe going alone?" There she goes again.

"Right. Look, I know we have a lot to discuss, and maybe we can also do that."

"No problem. But you should know that my fee has gone up to a hundred dollars an hour."

"A hundred dollars an hour? Why? Are you punishing me?"

"Yes," she says matter-of-factly.

Let's see, an hour each way, the show is probably around two hours, so that's four hundred. That's steep, but it is my life we're talking about.

"Okay. We should leave here by twelve-thirty."

Candy arrives at my abode at exactly twelve-thirty on the nose. I'd say she's nothing if not punctual, but in fact she's plenty of things. Maybe too many. She looks casually stylish and sensational as always, which serves only to mess up my conflicted mind even more than it already is. I greet her at the door wearing the same suit I wore to the Roddenberry memorial. Both Gates and Marina told me I looked nice that day, so I guess I want to look nice for Candy, too.

She checks out my ensemble as if she has a bad taste in her mouth. "Are you going to wear that?" she asks.

"Well, I thought I might, since it's on my body. Why?"

"You look like you're going to a funeral. Totally inappropriate for an afternoon event on a college campus. Go put on a sweater and some nice jeans."

No wonder I find her intriguing. She seems to naturally go right for my Achilles' heel. I've always been a sucker for being bossed around and humiliated. I toss on a light cashmere sweater and jeans and return to the front door.

"Okay?" I say, referring to my outfit.

"That'll do," she replies without much enthusiasm.

As I start to exit the house, she throws an arm across my chest, blocking my way. She quickly checks out the neighborhood, her eyes surveying the periphery, her ready hand poised to reach for that hidden revolver. Money very well spent.

"Let's go," she says, covering me the entire way to her classic Buick Regal.

She flips on the radio and tunes it to some Top 40 station. Not exactly my kind of music, but it serves the purpose of preventing conversation and avoiding what's known as the elephant in the car. When we arrive and approach the Beckman Auditorium, where the performance will take place, I spot some of my castmates out front, signing autographs for a sea of what are presumably fans. I sign a few myself and greet my friends before taking our seats. The entire house is sold out and abuzz with anticipation. Candy and I sit next to the wonderful actor Roger Rees, an old friend of Patrick's from the Royal Shakespeare Company. Roger rose to acclaim for his performance in the title role in *The Life and Adventures of Nicholas Nickleby* both at the RSC and later on Broadway. He is now in Los Angeles playing Robin Colcord, owner of the famed bar on the TV sitcom *Cheers*. The stage is bare, but for a podium and one chair. The lights go down briefly, and as they rise again, Patrick strides onto the boards, a well-worn copy of Dickens's immortal novel in hand. The audience of friends and fans gives him the typically American entrance applause, and then a hushed silence stills the room. After a brief pause, looking into the house with steely eyes, he launches into his performance.

"Marley was dead, to begin with . . ."

The crowd hangs on every word of Patrick's magnificent interpretation, and those of us who know Patrick well, as a colleague and a comrade, are every bit as mesmerized by his vocal versatility and range, his expressions, his facility with multiple characters—Scrooge, Bob Cratchit, Mrs. Cratchit, Marley, the Ghosts of Christmas Past and Present, and most enchantingly, Tiny Tim. As fine as Patrick is as Captain Picard on *Star Trek: The Next Generation,* he squeezes every emotion out of this text, out of us as well. And we're reminded just how much a man of the theater he is, and that the stage is where he is truly in his element. After a two-hour tour de force, he speaks his final line.

"God bless us, everyone."

The lights dim and the audience erupts in enthusiastic appreciation. When the lights come up again, Patrick stands center stage, his right arm raised high above his head, sharing his curtain call with the great novel he holds in his hand. Spontaneously, the entire theater jumps to its feet, with cries of "Bravo!" ringing out from every corner of the auditorium. Standing along with everyone else, I notice Roger scanning the auditorium, his eyes moving across the orchestra and up and across the balcony. Quietly, through the sound of thunderous applause, he leans in to whisper to me.

"So much love," he marvels. "So much hate."

I regard Roger with an ironic smile on my lips as I consider the events of my recent history and the compex truth in his words.

After the final curtain call, several of us make our way back to Patrick's dressing room for champagne and congratulations. The small area is quickly crowded with friends from both his past and present: Marina, Gates, Wil Wheaton, Jonathan and Genie, and of course Roger, as well as several crew members from the show. Having stopped to sign a few autographs on the way back, Candy and I are relegated to the doorway, but fortunately Patrick has plenty of bubbly on hand for the occasion, and a couple of flutes are passed our way. The good stuff, naturally. It's intoxicatingly festive being with such good friends on this grand occasion, and I find my shoulders dropping from around my ears for the first time in days. But just as a peaceful calm is beginning to envelop me, a young woman's voice whispers from behind my back.

"Hi, Daddy, it's Lal."

I scream like Janet Leigh in *Psycho*. And as a result, so does everyone else. All heads turn and glasses drop and smash as Candy springs into action, shoving me to the ground, grabbing the woman by the nape of the neck, and pinning her against the wall.

"Stop it!" the young woman protests. "What are you doing?"

"Spread 'em, bitch!" Candy commands as she pulls her pistol from a holster in the small of her back.

Coming to my senses, if indeed I have any left, I am able to better assess the situation. "Wait, Candy, stop!" I shout. "That's Lal! I mean, the real Lal! I mean, that's Hallie Todd, who played Lal on the show!"

"Back off!" she snarls. Candy is breathing fire through her nostrils, and I can see she'd rather put a bullet through Hallie than release her hold.

"Candy, please! That's the wrong Lal! She's a friend!" I plead.

Slowly Candy composes herself and, to everyone's relief, releases her grip on Hallie. A stunned silence overcomes the room except for a couple of muted *wow*s and a few audible exhales.

"Hallie, I'm so sorry. You . . . you scared me," I say, sounding like an idiot.

"I scared you?" she remarks incredulously as she rubs the cheek that has just kissed a cement wall.

Sheepishly I turn to the others and attempt to defuse the situation. "Hey, look everybody," I say, "it's . . . it's Lal."

There are a few modest titters and Jonathan attempts to support me with a generous laugh that eventually devolves into a cough when no one joins in.

Candy, completely unfazed by this human comedy, holsters her gun and throws me a look.

"Excuse me, I need to freshen up," she says, and pushes her way through the dazed crowd and into the restroom of Patrick's temporary quarters.

The room remains uncomfortably quiet until Hallie finally cuts through the silence in a polite but slightly shell-shocked voice: "Great show, Patrick. So glad I came." With that, she pivots and heads for the stairs leading out of the theater.

"Hallie, I'll call you!" I shout after her, kidding myself that there's some way on earth I'll ever be able to explain.

Most of the others rapidly down their Dom Pérignon and,

after giving Patrick a final congratulations, vacate the premises. I couldn't feel worse. Brutalizing sweet Hallie Todd and spoiling Patrick's triumph in one fell swoop. I try to apologize, but in his usual fashion, Patrick holds up his hand and in an effort to ease my embarrassment says, "Don't think about it another minute. You know I love a good drama."

Candy steps out of the bathroom and with no apparent compunction about her earlier actions, offers Patrick her congratulations. "Thanks for the tickets, Patrick. The seats were great."

As she breezes past me, she throws a "meet you at the car" over her shoulder. I give Patrick a final hug, filled with shame, friendship, and respect for his fine performance. Head hung low, I slink through the doorway, where I'm confronted by Gates, an earnest look on her face.

"Brent, you know I care about you, so in loving candor, I have to question your choice of women."

"She's my bodyguard," I object childishly.

"We know what's been going on," she says, placing a folded piece of paper in my hand. "This is the number of a friend of mine, a very good therapist. I beg of you, give him a call."

"Thanks," I respond, both touched and insulted at the same time.

When I get to the car, the motor is already running, and as I slide in and shut the door, both Candy and I avoid eye contact. Halfway home, I decide it's time to come clean, if that's a term that can ever realistically be applied to me.

"Candy, I think you're an amazing woman."

"Shut up," she snaps. "Just get to the point."

"Okay, okay. I think you're fantastic, and this time we've spent together—"

"You're ending it, right?"

"I want you to know how great this has been. And how much I appreciate the way you've taken care of me. I couldn't have made it through this without you. But yes, I'm ending it."

"Good," she says, flashing that million-dollar smile.

"Good, what?" I ask, confused.

"I was going to say the same thing. You're a peach, and I love hanging out with you, but you were getting too involved. It's suffocating. I'm just not a one-man girl at this point in my life. I enjoy playing the field."

Typical of my neurotic self, I feel like I've just been dumped, even though I initiated the dumping. I probably should see Gates's therapist.

"I hope we can still be friends," I say, employing that time-worn cliché.

"Of course, doll. I've never let romantic entanglements get in the way of friendship. I'm still friends with most of my exes. Hell, Jimmy and I had a wild affair, and now we're practically besties."

"Jimmy?" I ask, fearing the worst.

"Yeah, James Woods. Jimmy's the greatest. I worked for him for a little while when some crazy actress he'd been dating wouldn't take 'it's over' for an answer. We had this mad passionate—"

"All right, all right! I don't need to know about this," I object, taking the opportunity to cut her off for a change.

Well, that pretty much seals the deal. When this is all over, I'm definitely seeing that shrink. We arrive back home, and Candy reminds me that she's still on the clock.

She surveys the property, both outside and in, and determines the coast is clear. "Do you want me to stay?" she asks, ever the bodyguard.

"No, I don't think that's necessary," I respond, relatively certain of my safety and hoping to save a few bucks.

"Well, just remember, if you need me, I'm only a phone call away."

"Yeah, thanks, Candy, for everything."

She puts her arms around me and I hold my "friend," knowing in my gut that for once I did the right thing. She touches my face tenderly, as only a good bodyguard can, then leaves me standing there, waving goodbye, watching her car disappear into the late Hollywood dusk. As the sun rapidly vanishes, in a way singularly peculiar to the City of Angels, I'm struck by its metaphor to show-business relationships. Easy come, easy go.

TWENTY-SIX   ROMANCING THE STONE

AFTER LOCKING AND bolting all of the doors, I slip into a hot bath, hoping to soak away the effects of this afternoon's turn of events. Gulping down a few bites of a leftover TV dinner of Stouffer's Escalloped Chicken & Noodles, I decide to turn in early and catch up on some much-needed shut-eye. A slight twinge on the left side of my lower back makes it difficult for my mind to completely shut off, so I roll a fat doobie and suck down half of it, followed by a couple of Marlboro Reds. That seems to do the trick. I glide into unconsciousness, unconcerned about the nightly dreams that haunt my sleep.

Sometime after midnight, I'm jolted awake by a somewhat sharper pain where the twinge used to be. Convinced it must be related to stress, I smoke the rest of my joint and try once again to suspend my consciousness. But this time, no such luck. As I lie there, hoping Mr. Sandman will bring me a dream, the ache in my side grows dull and deep. Starting to get slightly concerned, I turn on the light, sit up in bed, and meditate, in the hope of finding my way back to sleep. I learned to practice Transcendental Meditation when I was in college. I paid a guru fifty dollars, a bargain by today's standards, for a secret mantra that would guide me in reaching a calm and stable state. Meditation is not designed to aid in sleep, but that's where I usually wind up. Somewhere around my fifteenth repetition of *om gam ganapataye namaha,* a sharp, stabbing intensity overwhelms me. The pain, coupled with the paranoia from the pot I'd just consumed, sends me into a panic. My God, what is this? What should I do?

I briefly consider calling Candy, but since we'd managed to end things with a shred of my dignity still intact, my ego doesn't allow it. Practically falling out of my bed, I manage to grab this afternoon's wardrobe from the top of my laundry hamper and clumsily get dressed. The emergency room at Cedars-Sinai Medical Center is only a few minutes away, and if I can stay conscious, I should be able to make it. Fortunately, I know the fastest route there. As the old saying goes, "Take Fountain." Driving erratically, I flash on a woman I dated for a time who, because of a myriad of ailments both real and imagined, insisted she was in need of emergency care at least once a week. It was like our home away from home. We were actually the hundred thousandth car to pull into their lot and as a reward were given free parking for the night. Talk about luck. Smoking that joint was probably not a good idea. Not only am I dizzy from the pain, I'm stoned out of my gourd. Arriving at the hospital in record time, I pull into the parking lot, snatch a ticket from the machine, and swerve dangerously into the nearest space.

By now the pain has accelerated to a level where I'm going to scream or vomit. I stumble to the front desk and do my best to check in, but by now my agony is so encompassing, I can barely speak.

"What seems to be the problem?" the attendant asks, devoid of empathy.

"I . . . have . . . pain . . ." I choke out, pointing to my left side.

"Please fill out these papers and bring them back to me."

"I don't think I can," I manage to squeak out.

She lets out an irritated sigh but finds it in her heart to take pity on me.

"Just fill out your name, birth date, and insurance provider, and take a seat till someone calls you."

The place is packed with people in varying states of physical distress, and I park myself in the only available chair, praying that none of the sick and miserable recognize me. Directly across from where I sit, an unkempt middle-aged man seems to be in a state of some sort of unspecified dizziness. His eyes periodically roll back in his head and each time, just before he passes out, snap back into what I can only assume is some sort of focus. On his most recent recovery, he notices me observing him. A familiar flickering light begins to shine in his previously lifeless pupils and a crooked smile appears as he withdraws his swollen blue tongue back into his mouth. He takes a deep breath in what I'm certain is a preparation for shouting my character's name when from across the room a voice calls out: "SPINER! BRENT SPINER!"

A young man in scrubs, studying a clipboard, saves the day, sparing me certain embarrassment.

"Here," I say, holding up a finger in case no sound actually came out of me.

"Come this way," he says, directing me into a room of hospital beds, each one separated from the others by curtains. After leading me into my own private cubicle, he tells me to remove everything but my underwear and socks and to put on a hospital gown, open at the back. Once accomplished, I shuffle like a geriatric as he escorts me to Radiology for an X-ray. Afterward, I'm guided back to my bed, where I lie in torment for what seems like hours. The pain has become excruciating. I almost wish for Lal to burst through the curtains and put me out of my misery. At last an intern enters, snatches my chart from the foot of the mattress, and asks, "Mr. Spiner?"

"I think so," I manage.

"Can you tell me your birth date?"

"I don't remember," I say, tears running down my cheeks.

"That's all right," he says, grinning, "I'd know you anywhere, even without the makeup. I love the show. I just watched an episode last night. It was the one where you built a daught—"

"Please, what's wrong with me?"

"Oh, yeah, sorry. Well, from your X-ray, it appears you have a kidney stone," he says.

"What! A kidney stone?"

He immediately pivots into medical school mode. "A kidney stone is a hard object made from chemicals in your urine. After it is formed, it sometimes travels down the urinary tract into the ureth—"

"Okay, okay, listen, I'm in horrible pain. Can you please—"

At that very moment, a nurse enters carrying a hypodermic, which she sadistically thrusts into my backside, bringing me almost instant peace.

"Ohhhh, thank God. So what do I do now?" I ask. "This isn't fatal, is it?"

"Not at all, Mr. Spiner. You're lucky," the intern says on his way out. "We have an excellent urologist on duty tonight. He'll be with you in a few minutes."

Since the pain has diminished to the point where I can more clearly take in my surroundings, I'm suddenly overwhelmed by that all-pervasive awful antiseptic hospital aroma. I detest that smell. For most people it can elicit negative memories of sickness and dying, but for me, it provokes a particularly disturbing personal recollection—not that sickness and dying aren't a part of it. My uncle, Dr. Nathan Cotlar, a delightfully eccentric human being, was obsessed with the notion that his sons, as well as my brother and me, should all become doctors. I had no real interest in the medical field, but being especially fond of my uncle, I humored his delusion. And so, when I was sixteen years old, he finagled jobs for me and his son Stevie, my best friend, as orderlies at St. Luke's Hospital in Houston. Stevie was assigned to the operating room and I worked in what was then the recovery room of the eminent heart surgeon Dr. Michael DeBakey. I hated every second of it. My job consisted of doing menial tasks like cleaning bedpans and transporting patients to their rooms when they had sufficiently recovered, if they recovered. It was tedious work, and given my naturally slothful disposition, I would've much preferred to be sleeping, but I tolerated it for my uncle's sake and for a little extra spending money. My purpose, on the other hand, was entertaining the patients, nurses, and medical students, giving them a show and maybe a laugh or two while selfishly making my own day go faster. I fancied myself *The Disorderly Orderly* and did my best to make Jerry Lewis proud. Plus, I looked particularly good in scrubs.

The worst part of the gig, however, was the sickness and dying. It had an overwhelming impact on my sixteen-year-old psyche, and too often I was forced to withdraw into a trancelike state in order to avoid the pain of things so real, so terrible. And though I had long before become a master at disappearing inside myself, there was no question that I was simply not cut out for this job. I knew it was just a matter of time until the jig was up, and subconsciously, I couldn't wait. The curtain fell on this episode of my life in an especially catastrophic yet darkly comic way. Surrounded by a team of doctors, an older gentleman was wheeled into recovery from the adjacent operating room, having just endured carotid artery surgery in the hope of restoring proper blood flow to his brain and thus avoiding a debilitating stroke. He was hooked up to various monitors, and the medical team circled his bed, keeping an eye on his progress. The head nurse—let's just call her Ratched—instructed me to take the man's blood pressure. After wedging my way between the medical team, I wrapped the blood pressure cuff around the man's arm, but before I could begin the procedure, he briefly regained consciousness, opened his eyes, and looked directly at me.

"Am I dead yet?" the man asked.

"Not yet," I replied brightly, in the misplaced hope of cheering him up.

This was clearly the wrong response, as I was instantly yanked away by the scruff of my scrubs by one of the attending doctors. "Don't you ever say anything like that to a patient!" he hissed, his manicured finger practically poking up my nose.

"Sorry, I thought—"

"You thought wrong!" he snarled. Turning away in disgust, he conferred with the rest of his team, and satisfied with the patient's stability, he and his crew left him in the care of Nurse Ratched and me. I'd barely recovered from my dressing down when she ordered me to take the man's temperature.

"But he's unconscious," I objected. "As soon as he wakes up, I'll do it."

"Take his temperature," she said icily, holding up a frightening looking object.

"What is that?" I asked with trepidation.

"This is a rectal thermometer. Just turn the man over on his side and insert this into his rectum."

I froze momentarily, then quickly searched my brain for an effective counter. I decided honesty was best. "Nurse Ratched, please try to understand. I'm just a little more than three years past my bar mitzvah. I don't even feel comfortable saying the word *rectum,* much less having to engage one."

"Don't be a baby," she spat without pity. "Turn the man onto his side, insert the thermometer, wait two minutes, then remove it.

I could see no way out, shy of crying or fainting, both of which seemed a little extreme even under these circumstances. I inhaled a lungful of air, rolled the man onto his side, and as delicately as possible, inserted the dreaded thing. I stared at my watch for what seemed the longest two minutes in the history of the universe, and when the time had finally passed, I reached out to remove the thermometer and found that he had rolled back onto his back. Oh shit. Fearing the worst, I nonetheless rolled him once more onto his side. Scattered on the bed were several glistening beads of mercury and what amounted to about half a thermometer's worth of broken glass. The other half was most certainly "where the sun don't shine." Chaos erupted in Dr. DeBakey's recovery room, so I took the opportunity to slip out, change into my street clothes, and catch the bus back home. That day marked the end of my medical career, except for the couple of occasions when I've played a doctor on TV. The smell in this ER is bringing it all back, and though my kidney pain has subsided, I'm feeling nauseous from the memory.

"Hello, Mr. Spiner," a sober presence announces. "I'm Dr. Urich. I'm a urologist."

"Urich, the urologist?" I ask, trying not to smile. "That's rather ironic, wouldn't you say?"

"Not really. It's actually quite common for one's name to be onomatopoeic. In fact, I know a dentist named Dr. Filer and a dermatologist named Dr. Flesh."

"Interesting," I retort, "but that's not onomatopoeia. I believe that's called an aptronym."

"Whatever," he says, dismissing my grammar lesson. "Mr. Spiner, you have a smallish kidney stone lodged in your urethra. As I'm sure you've noticed, that can be very painful."

"I've noticed."

"The injection you were given will probably last only a couple more hours, so I'm going to send you home with something that will help ease the pain when it returns. And it will return. This is a very strong narcotic called Percodan. I suggest you get into bed, drink as much liquid as you can, and take one of these every twelve hours. With any luck, you'll pass the stone in the next few days. But if you don't, I'm afraid surgery will be necessary."

"Oh, great," I say sarcastically. "I can't have surgery, I'm working all next week. And what do you mean by 'pass it'?"

"You'd eliminate it when you urinate. That's why I suggest drinking a lot of liquids. Although—"

"Although what?" I ask.

"Let me be honest with you, Mr. Spiner. The pain you've experienced thus far is a walk in the park compared to what passing a stone can feel like. It's probably as close as you'll ever come to experiencing the agony of childbirth."

Under normal circumstances, I'm basically a "glass is half full" kind of guy. And for a few hours, I'm even grateful that this kidney stone fiasco distracted me from the fact that a crazed fan wants to kill me. But as I pull into the driveway of my house at four in the morning, the glass empties completely, and I consider the possibility that Lal could show up while I'm delivering a jagged rock through my penis.

TWENTY-SEVEN THE ARMS OF MORPHEUS

WHATEVER WAS IN that hypodermic allowed me a brief pain-free sleep, but true to the doctor's words, I snap awake with the same agony that sent me to the hospital in the first place. I immediately pop a Percodan and writhe in my bed until it takes effect. It doesn't take long. Within minutes I'm higher than I've ever been in my life, and simultaneously as down, in the drug sense, as I've ever felt. It's as if my head is in the stratosphere, while my body has basically ceased to be. This is fantastic! Why can't life feel like this all the time? Sort of half hallucinating and half conscious, I begin having a conversation, out loud, with a shadow on the ceiling that appears to be moving in mysterious ways.

"Hi, God, it's Brent. How're you doing up there?"

"Not bad. Same old problems. What can I do for you?"

"Well, you know, ha, of course you know, but you know this stalker who wants to kill me? Did I do something to deserve this? This, this girl from a mental facility, uh . . ."

Then I start thinking about Grace, or Lal, or whoever she is and forget who I was talking to in the first place. I think it was someone important, but I can't quite remember who. And now I can't remember who I was thinking about just a second ago. Wow, I am *really* stoned. I think I'll lie here and enjoy it and watch TV. Maybe a movie. I love movies. I consider movies to be my best friend. Except for cigarettes, I guess. Although this Percodan stuff is starting to challenge both of them for the top spot. In my blissful confusion, I reach for the remote and spend a few minutes trying to determine where the power button is. Once I figure that out, I'm happy to discover it's already tuned to the Movie Channel. No telling how long it would take me to figure out where the channel buttons are in my current state. Even more serendipitous, they're airing *Key Largo* with Bogie and Bacall and Edward G. Robinson. I love this picture, especially for Bogart and Robinson and the great Claire Trevor performance. Not so much for Bacall. When I come across her in a film, I usually turn it off.

I had a bad experience with Bacall once. That's probably why I couldn't bring myself to watch *The Fan*. I was playing Konstantin in a production of *The Seagull* at the Public Theater in New York. It was pretty much an all-star production except for me. Christopher Walken, Rosemary Harris, F. Murray Abraham. During my curtain call on opening night, I spotted Bacall sitting in the front row. We both bent at the waist at the same time: I, to take my bow, and she, with her hands cupped around her mouth, to boo me, and to make sure I saw and heard her. Needless to say, she's not a fan of mine. But, to give her her due, I wasn't very good in that show. Nonetheless, whenever she comes on-screen in this movie, I boo. And even though, because of the pain, I can't bend at the waist, I get some kind of drug-induced satisfaction from it. Oh, here's the scene with Robinson in the bathtub. What a brave actor he was, unafraid to show ugliness to its fullest. He's like a gargoyle floating in oil.

Senõr Percodan is now working overtime and my vision is getting soft and blurry. Maybe I'll turn off the TV and just think—or try to. Searching for the power button again, I begin laughing, remembering a moment I hadn't thought of in years. The more I think about it, the more it amuses me. When I was a boy, Sol bought one of the first remote-controlled TVs ever made, the Zenith Space Command. Ironic that it was called that when you think about it. The remote itself was rudimentary, but cutting edge for the time. On-off, volume, and channels. When the TV shifted from one of the existing three channels to another, it made a peculiar sound: *Ch . . . chung. Ch . . . chung.*

None of us were allowed to touch the Space Command, not even my mother. If we wanted to change the channel, we had to get up and do it manually. Only Sol could command the Space Command. Our den and kitchen were one L-shaped room with a terrazzo floor, and when you sat on the couch, you couldn't see back into the kitchen. One night, while Sol was contentedly watching Ed Sullivan, I was rifling through an overstuffed kitchen drawer looking for something destructive, no doubt, when a penny nail dropped out and hit the floor. *Ch . . . chung. Ch . . . chung.*

The TV shifted from channel 2 to channel 11. Apparently, the nail hitting the floor created the same channel-changing frequency that the remote used.

"What the hell!" Sol shouted.

He pushed a button on the remote and turned it back just in time to catch the end of a Steve Lawrence/Eydie Gormé number he'd been singing along with.

> *There may be troubles ahead*
> *But while there's moonlight*
> *And music and love and romance*
> *Let's face the music and dance . . .*
> *Let's face the music and dance.*

While the audience applauded, I reached down, picked up the nail, and dropped it to the floor again. *Ch . . . chung. Ch . . . chung.*

"What the?" Sol asked no one in particular.

Looking to the heavens, I thanked God for this unexpected gift. The nail-drop scenario repeated itself seven more times that night and every night for the next week. He even brought in a television repairman, who after taking it apart could find nothing amiss. It drove Sol mad, but it returned to me the sense of autonomy he'd stolen when he came to live with us. Somewhere into the second week he caught me mid-drop and put two and two together. I was given the belt, of course, but it was well worth it. If anyone was to see me right now in my bed, my face contorted in hysterical laughter from this memory, they'd definitely think I'd gone crazy. Or that I was taking Percodan.

The television is still on, so I decide to grapple with the power button again in hopes of turning it off and taking a nap. But my attention is captured by the images on the screen. Since the holidays are near, a version of *A Christmas Carol* is currently playing. I think it's my favorite, the one with Alastair Sim as Scrooge. I've come into the movie when the Ghost of Christmas Past pays his visit. But instead of addressing Scrooge, he looks directly at me. My God, it's Sol, dressed in Victorian robes, his curly black hair glowing! Damn, could that man wear clothes. He stares at me with angry eyes and speaks in a harsh, rasping voice.

"I come to you from the past, Brent, to show you the truth!"

"Seriously, Sol, I really love this movie. Do you have to ruin that, too? Wasn't my life enough for you?"

"Oh, *wah, wah, wah,*" he says, "You always blame me, don't you?"

"Hey, this part of the story is supposed to be about showing me why I'm the way I am. I already know that. It's because of you!"

"I'm so sick of this 'Daddy hit me, so now I'm damaged forever' bullshit. That cornball stuff was already tired when they did the Rocky Graziano picture. You're a cliché!"

"You know what? You're as bad at being the Ghost of Christmas Past as you were at being a father!"

"Oh, for Pete's sake, take some responsibility. Sure, I made a few mistakes, but you were you long before I met you. Look inside, Brent. That's where you'll find the fear that tortures you . . . Look inside . . . look inside."

With that, he disappears behind a heavy velvet curtain. I have to say, that was very unpleasant, and I'm starting to question the attributes of this drug. Within seconds he's replaced by another figure, caped and dashing. Jesus, it's Patrick!

"I am the Ghost of Christmas Present," he intones theatrically.

"That's a different voice from the one you used in your one-man show. Nice touch."

"I am here to teach you about empathy," he continues.

"Empathy? I have empathy, don't I?"

"Of course you do. For others. But what about for yourself? You've allowed the past to dominate your feelings of self-worth."

"Well, surely you met Sol. He was just here. You must've passed him in the hallway."

"Forget about him! Take some responsibility!"

"Jeez, that's what he said."

"'When I was a child, I spoke as a child, I understood as a child, I thought as a child; but when I became a man, I put away childish things.'"

"That's from First Corinthians, isn't it? You know I'm Jewish, don't you?"

"Then let me put it another way. Grow some beytsim, as they say in Yiddish."

And he disappears behind the same curtain. I wonder what's back there. Probably some kind of changing room.

Suddenly a third figure emerges dressed in a black robe, its face hidden in the darkness of a hood. An unfamiliar woman's voice speaks.

"I am the Ghost of Christmas Future. I represent the fear of death."

"Do I know you?"

"Hello, Daddy."

"Lal."

"Of course, who'd you think it was? I'm expecting you, Daddy. Are you prepared to spend eternity with me? Soon, Daddy . . . soon . . ."

She begins backing away.

"Wait! Why are you doing this?"

"Soon . . . soon."

And she, too, disappears behind the curtain. My fingers finally find the power button on the remote and it clicks off. I lie here trying to understand what's happened, but the drug still scrambles my thoughts, and before long, I drift into the arms of Morpheus. Or Percodus, to be more specific.

TWENTY-EIGHT

FINDING GRACE

WRENCHED AWAKE AGAIN by the dull, debilitating ache in my side, I swallow another pill, and thankfully it soon takes effect. But it's different this time. It still eases the pain a bit, but my mind is clearer now, not completely, but more than I want it to be. I must be getting accustomed to the drug. What a disappointment. I'm weak and I feel like a sitting duck, yet somehow, I don't feel as frightened about Lal. Maybe I've gotten used to the fear, or maybe it's just the Percodan. Oddly, I'm almost eager to meet her. To finally face my fate, and in some way, I guess, to finally face myself. I'm so bored, just lying here, doing nothing. I haven't eaten for a while, but I don't have the energy to do anything about it. I need help, and the only person I can think of to call is Candy.

"Hi, Candy. It's your old pal. Long time no see."

"I saw you yesterday. Remember? We broke up?"

"Yeah, I remember, sort of. Listen, I wonder if you'd mind coming over? I could use some assistance."

"What's the matter? You sound strange."

"Well, it seems I have a kidney stone, and I'm in a great deal of pain. Not a lot right at this moment, because I just took one of these great pills the doctor gave me, but it's bad."

"I'll be right there."

She arrives about forty-five minutes later. Somehow I make it to the door to let her in, but she has to help me get back to bed.

"What took so long?" I ask. "Usually you get here in no time."

"I stopped at Cantor's to get you some matzo ball soup. And I bought some pajamas for you at a discount place next door. I hope they fit. If I'm going to stay here for a while, I don't want to look at you in your underwear all day."

"Wow," I say, "you really are a generous person."

"I'll add them to your bill."

"Then again—"

"I'm going to go warm this soup up. It probably got cold on the drive over," Candy says, as she heads for my kitchen.

I hate pajamas. There's no way I'm putting them on even though I'm paying for them. The phone rings.

"Hello."

"Hey, I'm glad you're there," says Cindy on the other end.

"I can't exactly say I'm here. At least not all of me. I spent a few hours at Cedars last night and I'm on a really strong narcotic."

"What happened? Are you okay?"

Nice to hear the concern in her voice.

"No, not really, but it'll pass." I chuckle to myself at my stupid little joke. "So is this call business or pleasure?"

"Business," she says.

There is a long pause while I wait for the news. Too long.

"Don't you know the rules by now?" She sighs. "ASK ME!"

"Oh! Right! Yes," I answer. "Did something happen? Do you have new information? What is it?"

"We found Grace."

I suck in an involuntary gasp.

"You did? You found her? And?"

"It's not the girl, Brent."

"What? Well then, who is it?"

"Are you sitting down?"

"No, I'm lying down! I'm in bed!"

"That's probably best," she says.

"Tell me!"

"It's the shrink. Dr. Sandra Ogilvy is Lal."

I'm totally gobsmacked. I feel dizzy. She seemed like she was on our side, trying to help. She's a doctor. A psychiatrist!

"The shrink wrote me all those death threats?"

"Uh-huh," Cindy answers with absolute certainty.

I still can't wrap my drugged mind around this. It's too crazy. "How do you know? How did you figure it out?"

"It's complicated. I'll tell you when you're feeling better."

"No you won't! You'll tell me right now!"

"Okay. Remember the orderly who left a late-night message

on your phone machine? Well, he got in touch with me. Grace was contacting him from time to time. They were friends, maybe more. He was concerned, so he gave us a tip that we could find her living in a crack house in an abandoned textile mill in Provo, Utah."

The girl was only eighteen, and the scene Cindy described in the drug house was lurid and sad. I found myself feeling sorry for her.

"She was scared and wanted to talk. She said she'd been living on the streets after the shrink kicked her out. Out of her bed, that is, not the institution.

"What? Whoa," I say, bracing myself for whatever was coming next.

"She said she and the doc had been 'unlocking the unconscious,' so to speak, for going on six months. They originally hit it off watching *Star Trek: The Next Generation* in the common room at night. In her therapy sessions they talked about the show intensely, in particular exploring the idea of the nonjudgmental but completely unavailable man, the sexy android Data, with the doc suggesting that perhaps Data wasn't actually a man, but a woman."

"That's ridiculous," I say defensively, "though I do try to stay in touch with my feminine side."

"She claimed the doctor became enthralled with all things Data, even more so than she was, and wondered if she could get you to perhaps make an appearance at the hospital. Maybe for Christmas. Grace also revealed that the doc was not her first shrink/lover, but she was the first shrink she'd slept with who looked like that. I asked, 'Like what?' And she said, 'like Glenn Close in *Fatal Attraction.*' It's true. I hadn't thought of it but she does look a lot like Glenn Close."

"You mean Dr. Sandra Ogilvy has tousled blond hair, piercing blue eyes, and cheekbones that could poke your eye out if she whipped her face around too fast?"

"Yeah, pretty much."

My mind did a fast flashback to the conversation I had with Rudy, the gate guard at Paramount, about the woman who showed up saying she was Wil Wheaton's tutor.

"Do you remember what she looked like?" I ask.

"Yeah, she was blond. Looked kind of like that actress . . ."

"Jodie Foster?" I offered.

"No, no, not her. The one who did that picture with Kirk Douglas's boy. Fatal Attraction. *You know, the one with a man's name."*

"Glenn Close?"

"Yeah! That's her. Dead ringer."

"Then the girl passed out," Cindy continued. "She'd been up on crack for close to four days without sleep and I figured it was just the drugs talking. I was all prepared to tell you not to worry. There was no way that poor girl could ever hurt you. But as we were leaving, I saw her address book and I swiped a page for a handwriting sample. It didn't match the bloody letters, Brent. It wasn't her. Plain and simple."

This is all so intense, I can barely breathe and I feel like I could have a heart attack. The pain in my side gets worse, and I consider taking another Percodan, but I think better of it. Enough with the drugs—I don't want to wind up in some Percodan house somewhere. Cindy continued with her revelations:

"I decided to go to Kansas City to see the shrink, to find out if she really was sleeping with the girl. Grace had seemed like a drug addict, like a lost kid, out of it, but something about her story rang true, and I couldn't shake it. I was wondering if Dr. Ogilvy exploited this fangirl's weak spot and used it to seduce her and make her own Duluth existence more interesting. If the affair was true, this was statutory rape. The girl was underage."

"And what did you learn?" I ask. I feel another sharp stab in my side, which I ignore.

"We surprised her at home. Every kind of person is different in their home than they are out in the world. Being in someone's home is like being in their mind. How comfortable is it? Is it tidy? Messy? Cluttered? Cold?"

I looked at my yard, a total disaster. Palm fronds everywhere from the Santa Ana winds, weeds, everything in need of watering. My gardener, Elías, had died of a heart attack six months ago. I hadn't had time to find another one. Didn't really know my neighbors to ask them for a recommendation. The problem with going over and saying hi and getting to know your neighbors is that then they get to know you. And these days, that just doesn't feel like something I want. More people knowing where I am, where I live, what kind of car I drive, who I'm sleeping with. These days I don't want anyone to know anything about me.

"So what did she say?" I ask.

"Again, she wasn't expecting a visit from the FBI. But in phone conversations she was expansive, open, friendly. When we sat down in her house, she was narrow, like a hallway, rather than open like a room. She was prickly, she was reserved. She denied the affair with the girl and said that she had hoped a female therapist could break the cycle that the girl had established in two other facilities with two other therapists, both men. She said Grace had seduced the other therapists, because she thought their aloofness was proof that they wanted her sexually. That she had been sexually abused by her stepfather."

"Shit," I said.

"Are you sure you want to hear the rest of this right now? You sound tired. I could call you tomorrow."

"No, for fuck's sake. I'm literally on the edge of my . . . bed."

"Ogilvy said she was hopeful that because she was female—a mother figure, not a father figure—Grace wouldn't transfer these same fantasies and fears onto her. But she said it seemed to cross gender lines, and it wasn't actually about sex, it was more about power. If you can seduce someone, the girl's mind told her, you can control them. So Grace invented a fictional seduction, Ogilvy said, with her. That's something we have to investigate further."

"Wow, that's a little too complicated for me," I say.

"We'd been in her house for quite a while, so I asked for a glass of water while I wrote up the notes at her coffee table. It's the oldest trick in the book, the water glass."

"What do you mean?" I asked.

"Really? Don't you go to the movies? You ask for a glass of water, smuggle it out, get a set of prints off the glass," Cindy said. "We ran her prints, and they match those on the letters to you. All of them. Ogilvy cleverly threw the attention onto Grace so no one would suspect that she was writing the letters."

"Jesus. Has she ever done anything like this before?"

"Not that we're aware of, no."

"Did you arrest her?"

"No, we didn't."

"What? Why the hell not?!!

"We try to avoid giving room and board at the taxpayers' expense unless it's absolutely necessary. Given her professional credentials, and because she's a first-time offender, we decided to let her off with a warning. Sometimes a good talking-to is all it takes."

"Where does one find comfort in this world?" I say mostly to myself, "I'm just curious."

"We went back to see her a few hours later, when the lab got back to us with the print ID, and I let her know, in no uncertain terms, she would lose her license to practice and face jail time if she ever wrote you or came near you again. Believe me, she was plenty shook up. I think you've heard the last from Lal."

"You mean, she's a goddamn deranged fan? This woman who ran a psychiatric institute sends pig penises and razor blades and bullets and blood-soaked death threats to actors out of what? She must be insane herself!"

"She's definitely not playing with a full deck. But we don't arrest people for that, either."

"She did all this just for kicks?"

"Far as we know. Yup. So, do you need any help over there?"

"Uh, actually, Candy's here. It's strictly business. I hired her to take care of me while I'm sick. She's heating up some soup for me right now. She can be very nurturing."

"Oh, you don't have to tell me. And that's a very important part of private security," she says sarcastically. "So I guess that's it for now on our end, Mr. Spiner. Brent."

"Okay, thanks for everything, Agent Jones. Cindy. Hey, you know I'll be bothering you for other reasons. Very soon. Before you can say Jack Robinson."

"I'll look forward to that. Feel better."

She hangs up. I can't wait to tell Candy that it's all over. She is not going to believe the shrink was the stalker.

"Kidney! I mean, Cindy!!! I mean, Candy! Fuck this Percodan."

I'm so amped from the news, I practically jump out of bed, head into the kitchen, and nearly trip over Candy, lying on the floor, unconscious.

"Candy!"

I bend down and check her pulse. She's alive, thank God. I gently shake her by the shoulders, and she starts to come around.

"*Mmmphh*, my head, chloroform. I'm so dizzy."

I notice the back door of the kitchen is open and a light drizzle is falling. There are wet footprints on the floor by Candy, leading into the backyard. And then the strangest thing happens. Instead of the paralyzing fear that would normally grip me, I'm filled with an overpowering rage. In the words of Howard Beale, "I'm as mad as hell, and I'm not going to take this anymore!" Though still wobbly from the drug and the pain, and despite the fact that I'm still in my underwear, I lurch through the door into the yard, bouncing off the doorframe on my way out.

"LAL! WHERE THE FUCK ARE YOU? DON'T HIDE FROM ME, YOU GODDAMN BITCH!"

God, that feels good.

"YOU WANT ME, OGILVY? COME AND GET ME!"

Something hard smashes against my left temple and I feel myself going down, falling on my face in the damp grass. A foot edges under my side and turns me over. And there she is. A bolt of lightning illuminates the tousled blond hair, the piercing eyes, and those cheekbones. I wish it was the real Glenn Close, but it's not. It's the goddamn crazy shrink in a beige trench coat, a rock in one hand and a twelve-inch butcher knife in the other. She drops the rock and straddles me, pinning my arms with her knees. The look on her face, like a snarling animal, says everything. She's here to finish the job. She raises the knife high into the air, exactly as Patrick raised his book at the end of *A Christmas Carol*. The strength has drained out of me, from the pills and the pain and the blow to my head, and I know with total certainty that there's nothing I can do to stop this madwoman from bringing that knife down into my body. I have nothing left. "Throat or chest?" she asks, accidentally similar to the way my stepfather used to offer "Belt or board?" But nothing feels accidental these days. Everything feels highly orchestrated and premeditated, as if I am the only one who doesn't know how the world works, how carefully every moment is managed and controlled for desired ends. I whisper to her, "If you really knew me, you'd know I can't make decisions," which is a crazy, illogical thing to say, but I said it with the last drop of power in my being. She grits her teeth and arches her back, and as the blade starts its trajectory downward, a blast rings out from behind her. A hole the size of a fist explodes through her forehead, spraying me with blood and bone and bits of her brain. Her lifeless body collapses onto my chest like an overstuffed sack of fan mail.

With great effort, I raise my head as best I can, but the blood dripping into my eyes makes it difficult to see. In the distance, wrapped in fog and drizzle, is the silhouette of a woman, her arm outstretched, smoke rising from the barrel of her gun. Candy? Softly, an unfamiliar voice speaks: "I love you, Brent."

It's exactly the way Philip Marlowe described being knocked cold in *Murder, My Sweet.* "A black pool opened up at my feet." As I drift into unconsciousness, a siren in the hills grows louder and nearer. And for a brief second, the woman momentarily comes into focus. As her gun lowers to her side, I hear myself answer her: "I love you, too . . . Loretta."

And then I fall into the black pool.

I'm walking with Sol on a Houston street. It's hot as hell and Sol is sweating through his jacket, something he never does. He's much too vain for that. We keep walking and the sweat spreads. He's not well. He starts to melt into the sidewalk, little by little. He's not dying, he's disappearing. Just before he becomes one with the pavement, he turns to me and says, "Try to understand. I thought I was doing the right thing. That's just the way we were back then." I know I'll never see him again, in my life or in my dreams. Oh, maybe a fleeting memory, but that's all. "One last thing, Sol, before you vanish into nothingness, that I want you to know . . . I forgive you." And then he's gone.

When I come to, I'm lying on a stretcher outside an ambulance, paramedics patching my dented skull. The rain has stopped and the skies are clear now. At first I think I'm seeing double from the blow to my head, but I'm relieved to find Cindy and Candy on either side of me, holding my hands.

"Candy, are you okay?

"Yeah, I'm fine," she responds, sounding slightly embarrassed.

"You were very brave. I'm proud of you," Cindy says, gently stroking my damp hair. "Brent, I know you're still woozy, but who was it? Who shot Ogilvy?"

I turn my head and see they're loading the doc's dead body onto the ambulance in my driveway. I look back at Cindy. I would give this woman anything.

"Did you get a look at the shooter?" she asks again.

"No," I say. Except this. I won't give her this. I'm not going to tell her. Not now or ever. I owe Loretta that much.

Candy tosses me a blanket and points to my crotch. "Here, buddy. Better cover yourself up."

Looking down, I see a large wet stain between my legs. While I was unconscious, I must've peed my underpants. That's the bad part. The good part is that with everything that passed on this ghastly night, so had the kidney stone.

EPILOGUE

PEOPLE OFTEN JUSTIFY a terrible turn of events by saying, "Things happen for a reason." I don't buy into that. I think awful things just happen. But whether the nightmare I experienced over the last few months occurred for a reason or not, insane as it seems, I feel better for it. I can't say that for everyone. Certainly not for Dr. Sandra Ogilvy. I managed to prod Cindy into giving me some of the details of the FBI follow-up on the case. They confiscated Ogilvy's computer and filled in a few of the blanks. On it were receipts for airplane tickets from Duluth and Kansas City to various spots around the country. That explained how the letters were postmarked from different cities. Some flights were to Los Angeles and one was to San Diego. She was at the convention, and at Paramount trying to get onto the *Star Trek* set, and obviously at my house more than once. They also found her journal. There was an entry about a letter she sent to me at the studio asking if I would come to the institute at Christmas. She had told Grace and the other kids that she was sure I would come, and when I didn't respond, it sent her into a psychotic rage. She felt humiliated and vowed revenge. I never saw that letter. Or maybe I did and ignored it, I don't know. I get so many kinds of requests that I tend to rationalize that I don't have time to answer them all. Which is true. Still, this is the first time anyone wanted to kill me for it.

Cindy also spoke at length to the orderly, whose name is Charles Hernandez. He'd already had bad feelings about Ogilvy because of her sexual and totally inappropriate relationship with his friend. It seems he was snooping in the doctor's office and saw a couple of the Lal letters she intended to send to me. It alarmed him, so he called me anonymously. By the time Cindy first went to Duluth, Grace had run away, allowing Ogilvy to point the finger at her. He kept quiet after that for fear of losing his job. He had been taking online courses for years to become a therapist himself, and he finally got his degree. He recently quit the institute and set up a private practice in Utah. Grace and he are now cohabiting, so that story has a happy ending. Then again, Grace is now sleeping with another therapist. Oh well.

I got one more letter from Loretta. It was a letter of apology. Not for the previous letters she sent me or even for killing Ogilvy. She said she was sorry, but she had to end our relationship. She was now in love with someone else. She confided in me that she'd been getting calls every night from President John F. Kennedy, and that he wasn't dead after all. And just to add insult to injury, she said his calls were much sexier than mine. Well, duh, it's JFK. Anyway, I wish those kids much happiness. Though I have to admit, being thrown over for a guy who's been dead for almost thirty years still stings a little.

I finally had my first date with Cindy. I took her to the Star Trek Christmas party, and afterward she came home with me and stayed the night. It was one of the greatest nights of my life. The next morning I woke up with the flu and was sick as a dog for the entire holidays. Both Cindy and Candy brought me soup, but since they were afraid of catching the virus, they left it for me at the door. By the time I got well, Cindy was already seeing someone else. Seems she met him at the Star Trek Christmas party. She said he was a Hispanic detective who retired from law enforcement to become a screenwriter. I don't want to dwell on that. I still see the Jones girls now and then for a meal, and even though things didn't work out with either of them, I wound up with a couple of good friends. And that's nothing to sneeze at.

As for me, I'm back at work and enjoying it more than ever. Who wouldn't? I get to hang out with my pals every day on a terrific show and make a damn good living to boot. And I feel that the events of my recent past have made me a better actor, more open and capable of connecting with my emotions. That's what I've always wanted. To be a fuller person and a better actor.

And I've come to understand so much about the fear that has dominated my life. It may have started with Sol, or maybe it was there before him, but something about the stalking brought all of it into focus, and at last I was able to set myself free and make peace with my demons. That fear is something we all share, whether it's fear of pain or loss or heartache or even the big one, death. It's all unavoidable, and what we fear most will ultimately take place. No matter who we are, the world will one day regard us in the past tense. So there it is, and letting it control you is a waste of energy. The only way to spit in its face is to let it inspire you to live life to the hilt!

I've realized one other thing as well. That despite this nightmare of a year with the pig's penis and the bloody letters and the crazy psychiatrist posing as my late fictional daughter, there is one absolute truth for all so-called celebrities. That finally, finally, where would we be without the fans?

ACKNOWLEDGMENTS

THIS STORY HAD been percolating in my mind for some time. At dinner with my friend, the inimitable writer Jonathan Ames, I told him my tale and somewhere around dessert he stopped me abruptly and said, "You've got to write this!" He then wisely offered that I might enlist someone to help and suggested an author who worked on two of his TV shows, Jeanne Darst.

Jeanne and I met at Little Dom's in Los Feliz, where I gave her a *Reader's Digest* version of my idea. She laughed in all the right places. This meeting was followed by several breakfasts at said restaurant, where she helped me organize and structure the story, and ultimately, the book. She continued to collaborate and inspire me every step of the way. Many of her thoughts and words are represented throughout the book. It's an understatement to say I couldn't have done it without her.

I'd like to thank the entire team at St. Martin's Press for guiding me through this new adventure. Particular thanks goes out to my editor, Michael Homler, for his continued optimism and good taste. And a special thanks to Rob Grom for his fantastic cover design.

I'd also like to offer gratitude to my representatives, Steve Smith of Stagecoach Entertainment, Albert Lee of U.T.A., and my attorney, Don Steele, for seeing this project to fruition.

I owe a sincere debt of appreciation and deep affection to my *Star Trek* family for allowing me to make them a part of the book and for being who they really are.

Thanks and love to my family, Loree and Jackson, just for tolerating me and allowing me to live with them.

Finally, I'd like to thank a couple of people who had nothing at all to do with the writing of this book. And although they are both gone now, I may never have the opportunity to thank them publicly for what they gave me. So, thanks to my singing teacher of long ago, Michael Lawrence, and especially to my acting teacher and mentor, Cecil Pickett.

Brent Spiner
Malibu, California, 2021

ABOUT THE AUTHOR

BRENT SPINER is an actor, comedian, and singer best known for playing the android Lieutenant Commander Data on *Star Trek: The Next Generation* from 1987–1994. He has appeared in numerous television roles, in films, and in theater on Broadway, Off-Broadway, and in Los Angeles. He currently has a role in the TV series *Star Trek: Picard*.